*Summer
Storm*

Summer Storm

June Lewis Shore

ABINGDON ° Nashville

SUMMER STORM

Manufactured in the United States of America

Library of Congress Cataloging in Publication Data

SHORE, JUNE LEWIS, 1930–
   Summer storm.

   SUMMARY: A destructive tornado that sweeps through a small Kentucky
community is only the beginning of the experiences involving fourteen-year-
old Vonnie and her household of family and friends during the summer of 1939.
   [1. Tornadoes—Fiction. 2. Family life—Fiction. 3. Kentucky—Fiction] I.
Title.
PZ7.S55868Su   [Fic]   76-41316

ISBN 0-687-40609-9

For Rue and Blanche Lewis

CHAPTER
1

The first day of summer seemed like any other day, although there were those who said they'd had premonitions all along. Mama remembered that Fred had been restless. He'd followed her from room to room, growling and whining; she'd nearly tripped over him a dozen times. My grandfather reminded us that he'd felt trouble in his bones and had told us so at breakfast. But, unlike Fred and Grandpa, I had no special senses which would have led me to believe that June 21, 1939, would begin a significant period in my life. After all, although Elk Run was billed as "The Biggest Little Town in Kentucky," it was not a place where big things happened. There was a record snowfall once and an outbreak of head lice at Elk Run Elementary, but in between those events whole years slipped by without incident.

Late that afternoon—I remember "Jack Armstrong" was just coming on—Mama had sent Mary Grace and me to pick pie apples. Mary Grace did not go willingly, which was not unusual. She had the kind of skin that picks up sunburns and rashes, and if she had her way, she'd hibernate all summer. But without the blotching, she was a beauty—at least that's what everybody said. Since we were the only girls in the family, people who saw us together felt duty-bound to compare us, and after a good long look, they nearly always announced: "Mary Grace is the pretty one, isn't she? But they tell me LaVonda's got the brains." Mama would say, at that point, that I was just a late bloomer; that after all, Mary Grace was nineteen—nearly twenty—and Vonnie was only fourteen.

Frankly, I didn't care if I never bloomed. I had sensible dark brown hair which I braided in the morning and forgot and ordinary blue eyes which saw me through my Sabatini books. I was a half-head taller than Mary Grace, a good height for grabbing apple limbs, and I was wiry enough to pull myself to the top of the tree. I was satisfied. But Mama was afraid I'd get my feelings hurt, even though I'd told her time and time again that if I thought I'd grow up to be like Mary Grace, I'd kill myself.

For the trip to the orchard, she'd swathed herself like a beekeeper with little more than her nose sticking out. "I just know my hair's not going to curl," she was saying. "The air's so heavy. It's like August out here. Is that a snake?"

I couldn't help snapping back, "Good heavens, Mary Grace. We're just going to the orchard."

I didn't expect a response. Mary Grace talked at right angles all the time. Now she was slapping through a swarm of harmless gnats and complaining about Pidd. "I don't know why Mama didn't make Pidd come instead of me. He's nine years old; he could do something."

"Dad took him down to the Yards with him," I told her. My father owned a lumber company, the Matthew Mercer Lumber and Hardware. My brother Pidd picked up scrap there and burned it for a quarter a week, a salary which got him into the Grand Theater on Saturday afternoons. Pidd didn't care what movies were playing but he cared very much about the serial, and Episode 17 was coming up: *The Masked Rider Meets the Challenge*.

Mary Grace moaned. "Why can't summer be over?" she asked nobody in particular. What she really meant, was *why can't the boys come back*. After graduation, most of them had hired on with a construction company. Now half the town was over in the mountains building a bridge instead of on our front porch doing nothing.

She continued to complain: When she got older, she wouldn't let herself go like Mama did. When she got her own house, she'd serve dinner in the dining room every night with candles. And she certainly wouldn't let a wheezing old dog like Fred come right into the living room when there was company. On and on and on.

The trouble with Mary Grace was that nothing about the present ever pleased her. But the future; now, that was different. The future was going to be absolutely glorious. Someday—meaning when she took command—everything would suddenly turn right. I couldn't have disagreed more; I never, ever wanted things to change. I liked everything about my life and I wished I could be fourteen forever. There was no fighting—the World War had ended wars for all time—and the Depression was over. We had a new car with vacumatic shift on the steering and there was a fresh coat of paint on the house. The curlicue trim under the eaves and between the posts never looked so white and sparkling. And except for an occasional errand, like going for apples, I had the whole summer to do exactly as I pleased.

But unlike Mary Grace, I held no hopes for the future. From September on, life for Vonnie Mercer looked grim. *When you go to high school,* that's all I heard at home. *Vonnie, you'll have to improve your penmanship, wear brassieres, go to dances, wear stockings, budget your time, get a garter belt, stop your daydreaming, speak up.* It was all too horrible to think about. A garter belt, for heaven's sake.

"And another thing, Vonnie"—Mary Grace was still nattering away—"If you'd wear some clothes, you wouldn't get so brown." She looked at my bare arms with utter loathing.

I ran on ahead of her then with the bushel basket bumping and scraping against my legs. I jumped high over dewberry vines and pounded through daisies that were just beginning to bloom and scattered the grasshoppers, still little and green, that whirred up in front of me. There was a distant rumble of thunder—"heat thunder" my grandfather would have called it—and I rumbled back at it. Finally, having run Mary Grace out of my system, I pulled up short at the pine tree at the top of the rise.

Ducking under the old gnarled limbs that swagged almost to the ground, I crouched along to one of my favorite hideaways, the mossy spot next to the trunk.

From here I could look back at our place and see it in a different way, as if it belonged to strangers. Everything looked neat. The garden behind the house was a perfect rectangle with no uneven curves where the plow had turned. The vegetables were up high enough to mark the rows, and across the far end at exact intervals poles for the runner beans stood tied into tepees. A flat patch of yellow-green, the lettuce bed, lay by itself at one side. (The lettuce was already bitter from the sun and going to seed, but that's what I knew, not what I saw.) Beyond the garden was a rambling whitewashed shed which housed hens and tools, the new car, and fifty years of clutter.

The house rose tall and straight above it all, its lightning rods pointing straight to heaven. I could make out Mama's snowball bushes in the back yard and the ramblers making splashes of pink down the fence row. Everything was beginning to bloom—the spikes of red sage next to the porch, the yellow zinnias around the pump—the whole wide world was about to burst, and it was almost too bright to bear.

I scooted around the tree and looked in the

opposite direction toward the Beckett place. I could see the wash—like tiny doll's clothes—flapping on the line, and a parked truck which looked like one of Pidd's toys for the sandbox. The door slammed and the driver—a miniature soldier—marched to the back fence and stood looking in the direction of our house. Finally, with shoulders squared, the figure advanced, growing taller, more human and then suddenly familiar.

Mary Grace came up just then. She was huffing and puffing and brushing back long, damp strings of hair that had worked themselves out of her curlers.

"Roman Budd's coming to see you," I told her. I knew it was Roman. Most of Mary Grace's boyfriends stalked about bumping into Mama's ferns; but Roman walked with grace and assurance, like a dancer with his moves carefully planned.

Mary Grace was panic-stricken. "He is not, Vonnie. You know better." She grabbed my arm as if force could make me turn him around. "Where is he? Can he see me?" I pointed across the hillside, and she took off her sunglasses and squinted. "Stall him, Vonnie. Just for a few minutes?" She was already pulling frantically at her curlers.

"Why should I bother? I thought you didn't like him."

"I don't," she said. "But I wouldn't want King

Kong to see me looking this tacky."

After making her say "please," I clambered down the bank to Elk Run, crossed the creek on boards Pidd had provided, and angled up across the hillside.

"Roman," I shouted, "How are you today?" I ran up to him and blocked the path.

"Very well, thank you." He spoke carefully as though he had to try hard not to betray his background. The Budds lived at the River Bottoms and were ne'er-do-wells even before the Depression.

He shifted to one side and, like a dancing partner, so did I.

"And how's Roxanne?" I asked. Roxanne was his sister who was in my room at school, though I really didn't know her well. She never stayed after school to play volleyball, and at recess she usually went off by herself with a stack of movie magazines.

"She's fine, thank you." His mouth tightened with impatience.

"Where are you working these days?"

For a minute, I thought he was going to tell me to mind my own business, but finally he said, "For Ed Weeks at the law office and on the farm with old Mr. Beckett."

Having run out of questions, I glanced down at the peck of apples he'd shifted from one hip to the other.

He looked directly at me. "They're paid for."

"Oh, don't be so touchy," I said. "Who said they weren't? There only happens to be two thousand five hundred varieties of apples grown in the United States. I merely wanted to see which you had in your basket."

He began to study me then, as if I were a specimen on a pin. "You're the smart one, aren't you?"

The trouble with a small town is that if you win a prize or two, you get branded as some kind of a genius. And if you happen to be a girl winner in a town where boys have won these prizes for a million years back, then you get to be a freak as well as a genius. People were always telling my folks that "the smart ones" were the first to go crazy, and wasn't it too bad that girls who were brainy ended up as old maids. Reluctantly I told Roman that I guessed I was the smart one.

He smiled then, and changed into a civilized human being. His blue eyes with the long lashes crinkled at the corners, a dimple deepened in one cheek, and there as a brief flash of very white teeth with a touch of gold at the side. "That's good," he said. "So am I. Now get out of my way; I want to see your sister."

"Mary Grace?" I was playing for time.

"Who else? You only have one sister."

I pointed toward the opposite hillside. Roman left without further conversation, and I called out "Mary Grace!" so she'd have one last warning. I really couldn't understand why I was being so nice to her. Maybe it was such a glorious day, I couldn't help myself.

After Roman was out of sight, I ambled back to the creek, settled myself on Pidd's boards, and eased my feet into the cold water. A school of minnows darted in all directions and the crawdads scurried to their rocks, but a snake doctor—the brightest, bluest dragonfly I'd ever seen—hovered over his mint bed, not giving an inch. There were patches of it growing thick around the rocks, and I grabbed a handful, buried my nose in it, and sat there sniffing the mint and watching the dragonfly and thinking. I did a lot of thinking out-of-doors because Mama couldn't bear it when I thought in the house. I think she half believed those stories about smart girls coming to no good end. Whenever she caught me staring out into space, she always quoted Longfellow—"Let us then be up and doing"—and then assigned me a bunch of busy work.

Right now I was thinking about Roman Budd. I wondered why he was bringing apples to Mary Grace when she'd much rather have a plaster pug dog with glittery eyes. I wondered why he wasn't seeing somebody his own age; Roman must have been twenty-two. I wondered about his job with Mr. Weeks. Roman always had some kind of job because his daddy, Old Beecher, was a wanderer. But Mr. Weeks usually hired law students and I couldn't see a Budd being a lawyer. The Budds did work like cleaning grease traps and hauling dead animals away. The thing that puzzled me most, I guess, was this: If Roman was bright—and he'd said he was—what was he doing hanging around Mary Grace?

Mary Grace had a perfectly good mind; she simply didn't care to use it. For example, we were riding in the car one night—my dad sometimes took us for a drive when there was no breeze and we needed to cool off—and Mary Grace admired the moon. "The moon sails along beside us," she said dreamily, "until we turn and then it leaps to the other side of the road."

"Well, you know," I had to tell her, "that the moon has no movement. None that we can see, anyway. It rotates around the earth, but you don't watch that from your car window."

She didn't answer me so I said again, "You do know that, don't you, Mary Grace?"

"What difference does it make?" she flounced back. "What good does it do anybody to know what the moon does at night or where it goes in the daytime?"

"But it doesn't *go* anyplace." I insisted. "It's there all the time and what you see at night is the reflection of the sun."

"Vonnie"—she was using her patient voice with me—"knowing how to make a pie with meringue that doesn't weep and a crust that is flaky is what's important. That kind of knowledge makes people feel good."

I told her that knowing about the moon made *me* feel good, and she said I'd always been strange like that.

Now, she was the one who was acting strange. She and Roman had either forgotten how sound carries over water or else they had forgotten me. I could have heard them perfectly well all along if I'd bothered to listen. Now, I couldn't help noticing that Mary Grace was not speaking in the tinkling, teasing voice she used with other boys. It was one I hadn't heard before, hesitant and fearful. And Roman, unlike her other boyfriends, did not speak of "spinning a platter" or "cutting a rug."

"Roman," she was saying, "I don't think Mama would let me go."

I thought to myself that, wherever it was, I surely didn't think so either. Mama didn't even know Mary

Grace was seeing him, not that she ever arranged a meeting. Roman just kind of jumped out at her at unexpected times and places.

"Mama only lets me go with boys she knows," she was saying. I had climbed to the top of the bank and was sitting behind a thin stand of sassafras where I could see as well as hear. I wondered if Mary Grace knew that the sassafras had three kinds of leaves on the same tree. I decided she wouldn't be interested.

Roman shook his head. "I'm not a boy, Mary Grace."

Mary Grace nodded as though she quite understood. She had flattened herself against a big sycamore tree, her hands to her sides, Roman stood with one tanned arm braced against the tree trunk. She looked up at him, then quickly looked away. "There're dozens of other girls you could go with," she said.

"But I don't want to go with dozens of others. I want to go with the prettiest girl in Elk Run; the one who wears clothes like a duchess; the one who sings like an angel."

"But Mama wants . . ."

He moved away from Mary Grace. Hands on hips, he almost shouted at her, "Mama, Mama, Mama. Don't you have a mind of your own? What does Mary Grace want?"

Now he flung both arms against the tree trunk, and Mary Grace was pinioned with a strong hand at both sides of her auburn curls. He repeated his question in a softer voice, "What does Mary Grace want?"

She strained toward him and looked up at him as though she were hypnotized. (I was half-hypnotized myself; this was almost as good as a picture show.) Then suddenly, she shook her head and darted out from under his arms. "Vonnie," she called, running toward the creek. "Vonnie, come quick. There's going to be a storm. Vonnie?"

I delayed a few seconds, not wanting her to know how near at hand I was. But the second time she called she sounded so close to tears that I came out running. She grabbed me by the arm and hurried— practically pulling me—toward the house. Looking back once I saw Roman still lounging against the tree, watching us with cool detachment, the peck of apples still at his feet. Mary Grace never looked back.

I was amazed at the change the sky had undergone in such a short time. The little gorge where I'd splashed was always shadowy. I'd fully expected to blink against the sun when I got to the field again. But the sky was no longer golden. It seemed to be measured into two equal parts: black at the top and irridescent white at the bottom.

"Can't you hurry, Vonnie?" Mary Grace was

pulling me through dewberry vines and down into ruts. Dirt clods had worked themselves into my sandals and stickers tore at my ankles, but still she charged on.

I jerked away from her. "Hold up, will you? I'm getting a stitch in my side." The wind had come up and I had to shout over it. "Those are cumulonimbus clouds, you know. Now, if we had warm, moist air coming up from the Gulf of Mexico and cold air coming down from the north . . ."

"Just shut up, Vonnie; shut up! The last thing I need right now is one of your lectures."

"Look over there!" I pointed toward the River Bottoms. A triangle had dipped down from the bank of black clouds. While we watched, it narrowed and lengthened and began to move. A tree limb crashed down behind us and I began to run, now taking the lead. With Mary Grace at my heels, I pounded past the garden and the sheds, through the gate, not stopping to fasten it, and stumbled up the back steps and across the porch. Mama and Grandpa were waiting and scooped us both in and bolted the door behind us.

It rained steadily and the phone went dead and then the lights went out. We had supper by candlelight, but Mary Grace, who set great store by candles, hardly seemed to notice. In fact, she didn't say two words all evening and was the first to go to bed. Usually she'd stay up after the rest of us and listen to dance music: Henry Weber's "Concert Revue" or Ray Sinatra's "Moonlight Rhythms." But, of course, with the radio out of commission, there wasn't much to do. By nine o'clock we had all turned in.

Up in my room, I sat for ages, comforting Fred, who was terrified of storms, and listening to the rain on the tin roof outside my window. The gutter must have stopped up; water spilled to the porch below and splashed along the steps. Because of the splashing and the noise from the poplar limbs scraping the tin roof and Fred's moaning, I didn't hear Mary Grace come in. She touched me on the shoulder in the dark, and I screamed and squeezed Fred. She screamed back and Fred barked. Then we shushed each other at the same time and ended up with a case of the giggles.

She sat down on the window seat beside me, scratched Fred's ears, and watched the rain for a while. Finally she said, after clearing her throat a time or two, "Vonnie, I don't think we should tell Mama about Roman Budd."

"We shouldn't?"

"No, she'd think I arranged the meeting and then she'd preach."

I didn't commit myself as to whether I'd tell on her or not. While I had an advantage, I wanted to find out some things that I didn't understand. "Tell me," I said. "Do you like Roman Budd?"

She gave the question considerable thought. "Yes and no. He's different, more manly, I guess you'd say than the other boys I know. But he's not nearly as comfortable as they are. I think he frightens me."

"Well, I like him," I told her. "He doesn't scare me one bit."

We were quiet for a while and then I asked her why Mama would mind her seeing him.

"Mama has people divided into two categories," she explained. "Nice people and others. The Budds are definitely others."

"How does she tell which is which?" I asked.

"I don't know what decides; I only know what doesn't." She stared out of the window as if she could see through the dark and drizzle. "It's not money. Lloyd Weber never paid for a Coke in his life, but he's quite acceptable."

"Maybe it's drinking," I said. "Old Beecher stays drunk all the time. When he's home, that is."

"No, it's not that. You've noticed that Miss Hattie has those little cough syrup pick-me-ups? Everybody knows what's in her bottle, but Mama only says 'Miss Hattie has a little problem.' "

"Do you think it could have something to do with church? Miss Hattie goes to our church and the Budds don't."

"Maybe. Or it might have to do with family; who your grandfather was and all that."

We never did reach any conclusions, although we decided to study the question further, and finally Mary Grace got up to go back to her room. I was surprised to find that I was really sorry to see her leave.

She paused at the door. "Are you going to tell about Roman?" she asked.

"I don't see any reason why I should."

There was a deafening clap of thunder. Fred howled, Mary Grace ran down the hall to her room, and I dived under the covers. I remember thinking as I drifted off to sleep that Mama never did ask us why we didn't get the apples.

CHAPTER
2

The next day I couldn't get away from the house until almost lunchtime. Electrical power had been restored and Mary Grace had the radio turned up so she could hear it in the kitchen. I remember that "Our Gal Sunday" was just coming on and the announcer was reminding us that this was the story that asks the question: Can this girl from a mining town in the West find happiness as the wife of a wealthy and titled Englishman? Mary

Grace pondered the question while she helped Mama cook for the disaster victims.

Elk Run did have a disaster—our very first. The twister had hit the River Bottoms with full force, clipped the south end of the town's business section, and then, being fairly well spent, done minor damage to the big houses up on the Hill. Daddy and Pidd were already out with the truck, clearing debris and moving furniture or people, whatever was needed. Grandpa was working at the elementary school where an emergency center had been established and where I was to take the food baskets if Mary Grace ever got them packed. She could do without my help, she said.

Once outside, I forgot to be insulted. I still couldn't believe the new landscape, and we weren't even in the direct path of the storm. The tall spikes of hollyhocks by the front gate lay fanned against the ground. The grass was littered with peony blossoms and a lake of yellow water covered the croquet court. Broken limbs swung from the trees and somebody's toy wagon had landed upside down in Mama's canna bed. Shutters dangled, fences were down, gates had disappeared.

Inside the school building, the scene was just as unbelievable. When school was in session, the new gymnasium was a sacred place. Now there were hundreds of people actually walking on the "playing surface," as our principal, Mr. Crenshaw, called it. He and Mr. King from the bank and my grandfather were seated at three long cafeteria tables placed across the front of the stage. The stage area, which had been off limits to students, was clustered with people lining up behind the three tables to declare losses and "list immediate needs." Those without homes were being assigned to families who had volunteered temporary housing.

I delivered my baskets to the Women's Auxiliary and pulled myself up to the edge of the stage, feet dangling. My grandfather acknowledged my presence with a nod as he rose to greet Mrs. Fingerle who lived in one of the big houses on the Hill. Mrs. Fingerle inclined her head briefly and they both sat down at the table.

"It wasn't my idea to come here, Everett," she said with a slight German accent. "Herschel thought there might be problems with the insurance if I didn't immediately report damages. You know my nephew, Herschel?"

"Yes, of course." Grandpa shook hands with Herschel, a big man, and offered congratulations. "I understand you graduated with honors. Business Administration, wasn't it?"

"Thank you, sir." Herschel had a soft voice and a

pleasant smile, and I decided that I liked him better than Mrs. Fingerle. He said that it was kind of Grandpa to remember his major.

Grandpa never forgot anything, but most people wouldn't have remembered Herschel's college career. He wasn't really a part of Elk Run, not having spent any length of time with us. Mrs. Fingerle, his aunt, had raised him, but that consisted mainly of getting him ready to go someplace else: to private schools and summer camps and Europe and New York. We always asked politely after his welfare, but nobody seriously considered him a resident.

"Will you be settling here?" my grandfather asked.

"After a brief vacation, I plan to go to the Mills," he answered. The Fingerle Mills, which turned out flour and cereals and related products, was the town's only industry. There was talk that Herschel would probably run the whole show someday.

Mrs. Fingerle was swinging her foot impatiently. I could have told her that no amount of curt looks or suggestive coughs could force my grandfather to hurry past the initial courtesies. He commented that we were happy that Herschel had decided to make his home in Elk Run—we needed stable young men—but it was unfortunate that he and his aunt had been so quickly unsettled.

Mrs. Fingerle did not give Herschel a chance to

answer. "I think you're supposed to record the extent of damages," she said. "At this point, I have no electricity, no phone, no water. The pin oak fell across the front of the house; I can no longer use my entryway. There's no roof over my bedroom. My Aubusson is waterlogged, and Papa's furniture sits there, swelling and buckling."

"My first concern, Marta," Grandpa said soothingly, "is to get you settled in." He began to thumb through his lists.

"She didn't sleep last night," Herschel said. "I wanted her to take a sedative, but she refused."

I decided that Mrs. Fingerle didn't look like a woman who'd spent a restless night. In fact, she didn't look like any other woman I knew. Her legs—I couldn't help noticing since I was at eye-level with them—were as slim as Mary Grace's, although Mrs. Fingerle was Grandpa's age. Most ladies that old had big solid legs encased in thick, red-brown stockings and sensible shoes with sturdy square heels. But Mrs. Fingerle wore sheer hose, long narrow shoes with slender heels, and a gray linen suit, untrimmed and unwrinkled. Her hair was waved back in ridges as even as those in an ad for setting gel and there were tiny pearls at her ears.

"I suppose we'll get rooms at the boarding house," she told my grandfather.

Grandpa told her that Kate had rented everything in sight.

"Then we'll have to go to the city," she decided. She'd gathered up her papers and her purse and was putting on white gloves.

"I think it might be difficult for you to conduct the business of repair and refurbishing from so great a distance," Grandpa said. "Let's study the situation." He was stroking his chin which meant he was already in deep thought. He was probably thinking that unlike most people, Mrs. Fingerle had no relatives to stay with; she was the last of her family, except for Herschel. Also, not having been folksy with the people in Elk Run, she had no close friends to call upon. She didn't attend church in town—each Sunday she drove thirty miles to the Lutheran church in Whitehall—and she evidently didn't take any interest in the local women's clubs. The Elk Run Literary Society, the Friends of Missionaries, the Pioneer Sewing Circle, and the Good Time Club had all met at some time or another at our house, and I never remember seeing Mrs. Fingerle at any of the meetings.

"Marta," my grandfather said, "I offer you the hospitality of my house."

Sometimes I forgot that our house really belonged

to Grandpa, and that we'd only moved there after my grandmother died.

"My daughter and her family would be most pleased to have you," he added.

Just then little Franklin Delano Budd, one of Roman's cousins I guess, ran up onto the stage and across it, his mama right behind him. "Frankie Del Budd," she yelled, "just you wait till I catch you." She went pounding down the other set of steps at the far side of the stage with Frankie well in front. A baby began to cry at the back of the gym.

Mrs. Fingerle sighed, and I noticed that up close she really did look tired, especially around the eyes. She kneaded her brow with a slender hand that flashed with diamonds when it caught the light.

She smiled wearily and let the hand rest briefly on Grandpa's arm. "You're very kind, Everett. Always were. When will it be convenient for me to come?"

Herschel insisted that he'd take rooms in the city but Grandpa said, "Nonsense. Your place is with Marta. We have plenty of room."

They were discussing arrangements when I scooted off the stage and made my way to the cafeteria. Food contributions had poured in from all over town, and the Women's Auxiliary were hard pressed to keep up with all the bowls of potato salad and the rings of gelatin and the hams marked off in little diamonds. There was a separate table for cakes, and I was pleased to see that Mama's coconut layer stood taller than the rest.

I got in line. I figured Mama was too busy at home to do more about lunch than to say, "Oh, Vonnie, get yourself something from the box." (We'd had the refrigerator with the big motor up on top for several years, but Mama still called it an icebox.)

"Vonnie?" I heard my name being called. "Over here, Vonnie."

It was Roxanne Budd from my class. She never had anything to do with me at school, but at the moment I was the only one around who was anywhere near her age. She probably looked a lot older with her bleached hair worn in a pompadour and her plucked eyebrows, but she was an eighth-grade graduate, just like me.

Her dark eyes flashed with excitement. Usually she was kind of stuck up, but now she began to talk right away. "Did you get hit by the tornado? We did. Sit down. I'll tell you about it." She was at one end of the table by herself, but the places were filling up fast as more and more people drifted in from upstairs.

"The noise," she said, "was like a mighty freight train. There was the sound of a whistle first, like a scream, then there was a deafening roar."

"No sound," somebody at the other end of the table said. "It just came on us unannounced."

The whole table erupted into an argument as to how it really was with Mr. Van Hoose holding that it wasn't even a tornado—"wrong time of year for tornados"—and Buford Johnson saying he knew a tornado, by George, when he saw one. There was a difference of opinion as to when the storm hit and, with that settled, everybody had to tell what they were doing at the time. Paradine Carr said that lucky for him, he'd just gone down to the cellar to check on a batch of wine he'd set. Brother Riggs, who was in town holding a revival, said that evidently God had spared Paradine for some special, heavenly purpose.

Conversation stopped at that point. I suppose people were having difficulty getting used to the idea of Paradine being an instrument of the Lord. (Paradine was the closest thing we had to a juvenile delinquent.) During the lull, Roxanne told me that her house had been blown "clean away." She and Mrs. Budd had been outside trying to find poke that was still tender, and her ma had pulled her down into a gulley. They had lain there with the roof sailing over their heads and the furniture crashing into the trees. "What a show!" she said in admiration. "What a wind!"

"Shame on you, young lady." Brother Riggs was outraged by Roxanne's enthusiasm.

I would have slid through a little crack in the floor if he'd talked to me like that, but Roxanne wasn't intimidated. "Well," she said, "nobody got killed, did they?"

Brother Riggs was taken aback. "Think of the destruction," he said.

"The River Bottoms? That's no great loss, I reckon." She went right on calmly chewing her stuffed celery.

I had to admire Roxanne's spunk. The worst thing a child could do in my family and in most of the families I knew was "to talk back." She had done it and the sky hadn't fallen in. Of course, I noticed the shocked look that passed between the adults at the table, but if Roxanne noticed, she certainly wasn't disturbed by it.

"Where will you go now?" I asked her.

"Don't know. Your Grandpa's put most of the people from the River Bottoms out at the Methodist campground. I think it's full now. Do you want your deviled eggs?"

I shook my head—they weren't like Mama's; too much vinegar—and Roxanne scooped them off my plate and popped both halves into her mouth at once. "Roman says we aren't going to move back to the

Bottoms," she said, still chewing. "He's going to build us a house somewhere."

"Do you think he really will?"

"Oh sure. Like Ma says, Roman's a fighter. He's hell-bent on improving himself, and he never gives up. Now Ma, she rolls with the punches; never gets in a flap about anything. Ma's too easygoing. Me? I'm somewhere in between."

I was waiting with rapt attention for more revelations, but then she turned the tables on me. "How is it in your family?" she asked.

I gave the matter careful thought, but nothing came to mind. Finally I had to admit that I just didn't know. "I never thought of my parents as people," I told her. "I mean *real* people, *different* people."

She looked at me critically, and I suddenly wanted to win her approval very much.

"I suppose you'll understand people better when you get older," she decided. "I'm sixteen. How old are you?"

"I'm fourteen. But I'll be fifteen in September."

"Do you smoke?" she asked.

I knew a bolt of lightning would come down through the cafeteria and strike me dead if I lied, so I had to admit that I didn't.

"It's just as well at your age," she said. "I wouldn't advise it."

We parted company when we got back up to the gym. Roxanne went off in search of cigarettes and I joined my dad and a group of men from the Yards. They were talking estimates and repairs and board feet and two-by-fours. Remembering how Roxanne had described her family, I tried to think of my father as a person other than my father. I knew what he looked like: a big man with muscles in his arms, a ruddy face from working outside, and short, sunbleached hair. I compared him with the other men and decided that he looked kinder than the rest, but whether my dad—or Matthew Mercer, as I was trying to think of him—was, in general, happy or sad or angry or disappointed, I really didn't know.

I heard Pidd whistling for our cousin, George Allen Comstock, or "Chuffy," as we called him. Two longs—that was Jack Armstrong's Whistle Code for "Important news: Meet me at once." Pidd caught sight of me and gave four shorts, meaning, "We're being watched." When Pidd sent off for a radio decoder ring or any kind of secret communicator, it usually took me less than an hour to break the code. But it took him months to figure out that I was on to it.

My grandfather stood up on the stage, peering out over the crowd of people milling about the gym. I looked at him carefully, thinking again of Roxanne's assessment of her family, and decided that he didn't look anything like my dad. There was no reason he should (they weren't related, Grandpa being my mother's father), but it struck me as odd that two men in the same household should look so different. Grandpa—or Everett Allen Comstock—was a stately man. He had lots of neatly combed silver-white hair, he was tall and thin, and he always wore a dark suit with a vest. He looked like a school principal, which he was before his retirement; in fact, lots of people still called him "Professor Comstock." For the first time in my life, I wondered if he liked all of us living in his house. I wondered if he minded when Mary Grace was in one of her snarky moods, or when Pidd insisted on listening to the "Green Hornet" instead of "Information Please." I couldn't think of anything offhand I did that would displease him, unless it was the harmonica. He might have grown tired of "Red River Valley," but I'd been practicing a new song for several weeks now.

"LaVonda"—Grandfather caught my eye and motioned me onstage—"I think you'd better go home and tell your mother to prepare for company." He looked slightly uncertain as he spoke, which was not at all like him.

"Yes. I heard. Mrs. Fingerle and Herschel are coming."

"That's right. And Mrs. Budd and her daughter will also be staying."

I looked at him in surprise.

"There's plenty of room, Vonnie. We must, of course, extend every courtesy to those less fortunate than we."

"Mrs. Fingerle is less fortunate?"

"Indeed she is, LaVonda. Now run along. Your mother will be needing you."

When I passed Pidd on my way out of the gym, I had a strong impulse to whistle two longs for "Important news," but I resisted. This last code was only two weeks old.

As Grandpa had told Mrs. Fingerle, we had plenty of room for company. All the houses in our neighborhood had second stories and wings and built-ons. And Mama had enough bedding to sleep an army. In the walk-in closet in the hall there were stacks of pillow cases with tatted edges and embroidered designs, and two shelves of quilts: *Log Cabins*, *Doves in the Window*, *Turkey Tracks*, and *Double Wedding Rings*. There was certainly food enough. Ever since the Depression Mama had hoarded food. She bought canned milk by the case and sugar by the hundred pounds, and although we had a fruit cellar lined with home-canned vegetables, she was already canning more. The dust in our house was never allowed to settle, the sitting room was always presentable, and Mary Grace kept peonies and orange blossoms in the front hall.

So having company should have been fine. Yet Grandpa had looked worried. Several days back, I wouldn't have thought about it one way or the other, but since Roxanne had nudged me into thinking about the family, I began to wonder how we would react to our unexpected guests and how they would react to each other. I wondered how Mrs. Fingerle and Mrs. Budd from the Bottoms would get along, and Roxanne and I, and Herschel and Mary Grace— that could be interesting—and Roman Budd and Mary Grace, and Grandpa and Roxanne, who wasn't afraid to talk back. There were all sorts of intriguing combinations, and I really couldn't predict what might come of them.

CHAPTER
3

Mrs. Budd was the first to arrive. "Call me Sadie," she said. "Nobody calls me Mrs. Budd except my old man." She laughed so heartily that Fred came rushing from the kitchen, growling and barking, and had to be chased back in again.

I decided on the spot that I liked her. I liked her liveliness and the way her black button eyes darted from one part of the room to the other, from one person to the next. Her cheeks were ruddy, her hair stood out from her head in crinkly little curls; even the bird on her hat looked as if it were about to take flight. It occurred to me that Roman had the same energetic quality, only in him it was not so good-natured.

"Now, Edna, what can I do to help?" she asked. "I'm no stranger to work."

"Nothing at all," my mother said. "Just get some rest, though I know it's hard to sleep in a strange bed."

"Lord, honey, I could sleep in a briar patch. Roxanne, you bring in the grips." Roxanne left sullenly, her *huaraches* flapping hard against the floor.

Mama had dispatched Pidd to help while Mrs. Budd apologized for not staying up to visit with us. "I have to admit it'll be good to get out of these shoes. Look at that, would you?" She held up a leg and turned it from side to side so we could observe the swollen ankle. All of us looked except Mama, who didn't admit to having feet.

Mrs. Budd winked at me and nudged me in the ribs. "You know, Vonnie, if these old feet didn't have so much to carry, they might hold up better."

I laughed with her, mostly because I was pleased that she'd remembered my name. And she had spoken to me specifically. Usually adults—strangers, anyway—just asked me what grade I was in and let it go at that.

Pidd came in carrying a large cardboard suitcase tied with ropes. Roxanne carried two shopping bags, one of which was spilling out a garter belt.

"Vonnie will show you to your room," Mama said, deftly tucking in the offending garment. "I'll come up later to see if there's anything you need."

"Well then," Mrs. Budd called from the bottom of the stairs, "good night."

"Sleep tight," Roxanne said, quick as a wink.

"Don't let the bedbugs bite." Mrs. Budd laughed merrily—evidently this was a bedtime ritual between them—and both followed me up the stairs. I looked back when I got to the landing and saw Mama cringing, her eyes closed. I know the mention of bedbugs must have hurt her, but she still managed to wish the Budds "pleasant dreams." I think she got her good manners from Grandpa.

I told Roxanne I was glad she was staying—which was the truth instead of manners—and she said she was, too. She said after she got her beauty sleep, we'd do something interesting. I told her I had Princess Elizabeth and Princess Margaret Rose paper dolls (I hadn't played paper dolls since I was ten, but I thought she might be interested in fancy clothes). I also had a Ouija board and a Game of India and books. Big Little Books, I hastened to add. I knew from school that she wasn't keen on the other kind.

She said she thought she could find something better than that for us to do.

Pidd and I managed to listen to the radio for a little while. Mama said we had to turn it off as soon as we heard the Fingerles. We were at the part where the Green Hornet and Cato were trapped in a vault by the Dunham Gang—there was no possible exit—when we heard Herschel's Deusenberg. From behind the curtains, we watched the luggage stack up outside that long, sleek, fantastic car: matched sets and leather hatboxes and Herschel's heavy calf suitcases with stickers from all over the world.

"Mama," Pidd said. "They're going to stay for years."

"Hush, Pidd. Don't you dare say anything like that before them." Mama always anticipated our social breaks before they happened.

Mrs. Fingerle knew all of us by sight, but Herschel had to go through the formalities of being introduced. As he shook hands with Daddy and Grandpa and nodded to Pidd, I watched Mary Grace come to life. All evening she'd sat in her chair, idly buffing her nails or thumbing through magazines. Now, at the sight of Herschel, she raised up out of her boredom like a mummy from the grave: first the smile, then the toss of curls—she was wearing it long like Brenda Frazier, "Debutante of the Year"—and finally, the arrangement of the body: legs crossed at the ankles, head tilted upward, hands demurely clasped.

She was wearing a moss green dress with a gathered skirt, a style which made her waist look smaller than it really was. The neckline was cut low and round to show off her neck and shoulders. Her skin was creamy by lamplight—the freckles masked with makeup—and her hair shone like copper. Even though it was supposed to be combed back and down, little ringlets were working themselves out around her hairline. I saw that Herschel was noticing this too.

Mama was offering Mrs. Fingerle the easy chair.

"No thank you, Mrs. Mercer. This will do." She sat on a Victorian side chair that belonged to my grandfather. It was so hard and sticky that those who sat on it were forced to sit up straight, which probably accounted for his good posture. Mrs. Fingerle seemed comfortable enough.

"We won't be troubling you long," she said. "I've already spoken to your husband about repairs."

My dad looked troubled. "Mrs. Fingerle," he said,

"we'll get to the work as soon as we can. Of course, we'll put up a temporary roof covering right away. But after that . . . "

My mother interrupted. "Matthew's the best in the business. He'll get you squared away in no time."

My dad resumed talking where he'd left off. "We'll have to take the work according to priority. Those with small children or sickness ought to get moved in first. Then those down at the Methodist Campground need to move back. Those facilities aren't great."

"But those are the River Bottoms people," my mother half-whispered.

"Yes, they are." Papa's voice grew quieter and there was a set look to his mouth.

My mother said cheerily that, no matter, she was sure Mrs. Fingerle would be back among her lovely things in a matter of days. Our visitor smiled wearily, not seeming at all interested in the exchange between my parents. "If you'll show me to my room," she said. This time Mama led the way.

Mrs. Fingerle was assigned to the first floor spare room directly underneath Roxanne and Mrs. Budd. Herschel would go to Grandpa's quarters, which was through the sliding doors off the living room. Grandpa had his own entrance from the side drive which led into a sitting room lined floor to ceiling with books, a big bedroom, and a smaller one that doubled as an office.

Dad went to put our car away and that left Herschel, who was staring at Mary Grace; Pidd and me, who were staring at Herschel; and Mary Grace, who was staring dreamily into space. After careful assessment, I decided that if I had to choose one word to describe Herschel it would be "comfortable." He was stocky without being fat, well-groomed but not prissy, good-looking but not movie star handsome like Clark Gable or Errol Flynn. He reminded me of a sepia photograph. He had soft brown eyes, sand-colored curly hair and a bushy mustache, and a light brown suit that never wrinkled. I don't know what it was about the Fingerles but they never wrinkled. Maybe rich people just don't.

Herschel cleared his throat and said to my sister, "Perhaps you'll like to drive out with me, Miss Mercer. It's such a warm evening."

Miss Mercer said that would be lovely, but she'd have to ask her mother.

"Allow me," Herschel said.

When Mama came back from settling Mrs. Fingerle, he jumped up politely and made his request. "It's still early and we shouldn't be out too long."

Mama hesitated, from force of habit, I suppose. I could tell that she approved of Herschel. She usually cross-examined Mary Grace's young men, but she hadn't asked Herschel a single question.

He added quickly, "Perhaps the children would like some ice cream. I think there's a stand out by the park."

Mary Grace looked startled, Pidd looked greedy, and I tried to look indignant. I didn't appreciate being lumped with Pidd as "children." But when Mama gave her permission, I decided that I could be just as indignant in the car as I could at home. We didn't have ice cream all that often.

Pidd begged to sit up front between Herschel and Mary Grace so he could help shift the gears—"Jeepers, what a car!" he kept saying—but Mary Grace thought he could get more air in the back seat. We both rolled our windows down but even with the cool air rushing in we could still hear the conversation in the front: "Oh, do you like Mickey Rooney, too?" "Do you like the *Thin Man* pictures?" "Do you like Tyrone Power? Sonja Heine? James Cagney? Alice Faye?"

I think they intended to go through the Hollywood phone book, star by star.

The storm damage was much more fascinating. The wooded hill to the left of the road looked as if a giant lawn mower had gone beserk across its side. The houses to the right were missing shingles and shutters, but they'd get fixed; my dad would see to that. But the trees? It would probably take them a hundred years to grow back. The big old oak that had stood by the park entrance for as long as I could remember was down, its roots blocking the road to the Lookout. If we were having a Sunday school picnic or collecting leaves for science notebooks, we always met by the oak tree at the entrance. We parked by the big gaping hole where the roots had been and I tried not to look down.

It was too soggy for the usual Friday night softball game, but the refreshment stand was open. Herschel bought us cones, and Pidd and I sat at one of the park tables trying to catch the drips before we started in on the scoops. Mary Grace and Herschel had moved on up the path. They were out of earshot but I could see them—Herschel had spread out his handkerchief on a low stone wall and had lifted Mary Grace up on it. I suppose he didn't know that she could have jumped up there herself.

Pidd said that Herschel must be rich.

"How come?" I asked.

"Well, how often do you get triple dips?"

I was too busy to talk, but I nodded my head to

show that Pidd was right. From someplace back in the trees, an owl hooted.

We worked the cones down to manageable little mounds and then Pidd said out of the blue, "Do you ever get scared, Vonnie?"

"Scared of what?"

"Oh, I don't know. Ghosts or wild animals. Things like that."

"Well, I guess everybody's been scared some time or other. Do you?"

"Yeah. I have bad dreams about tigers. I think I'm screaming for help, only when I wake up I'm just making little squeaks. Then I try not to go back to sleep so I won't see them again."

"Why don't you wake up Mama?"

Pidd started crunching the cone. "Because," he said between bites, "I'm too big."

"Well, I get scared, so scared before a contest that I could just die."

"Everybody gets scared before speeches. But tigers I see in the night aren't even real. Once the light from the hall was shining on the eyes of that old bear of mine and I thought it was a tiger. I couldn't move for the longest time. Even after I figured out what it was, I couldn't move."

We finished our cones and I kept thinking about Pidd being so scared and not wanting to tell because he was too big. I remembered him back in the spring after the early rains. The creek was swollen and the current was swift and rolling. Pidd jumped on a log and rode the current, maybe half a mile. I ran along the bank screaming at him as long as I could. When he was out of sight, I still stumbled along after him. Finally, he grabbed a sycamore limb and hand over hand came back to the bank. I'd thought he was going out to the river. When he finally came running up, I was so glad to see him but so mad that I hauled off and hit him—hard.

He said he was going to tell Mama and I said I'd tell about him being in the creek if he did, so neither one of us ever told. Mama thought Chuffy had given him the black eye and we never set her straight.

"Listen, Pidd," I told him. "When you have those bad dreams, you come in and wake me up, you hear?"

"Well, I probably won't have them anymore," he said.

Herschel and Mary Grace came ambling down from the wall, taking their own sweet time about it. Herschel was telling a story. He stopped every few steps and made gestures with his hands, and Mary Grace laughed and oohed and aahed. "A Conga line right through the lobby?" she squealed. "I just can't believe it." She was so weak from laughter she had to rest against a tree. I remembered her with Roman at the sycamore tree and wondered if she ever thought about that.

On the way home I asked Mary Grace why Roman didn't come with the rest of the Budds.

"Well, I certainly wouldn't know, Vonnie. You'd have to ask Mrs. Budd about that, I reckon."

"I know where he is," Pidd said. "He's sleeping in Mr. Beckett's barn. He's working shares for Mr. Beckett. Mr. Beckett gave him some land, and Roman's gonna build a house for his mama there."

I asked Pidd how he knew all this.

"Because Daddy and I were talking to him. He's getting some lumber and gravel and stuff from the Yards."

"What's he using for money?" Mary Grace asked.

"Oh, he's got money," I told her. "He works for Mr. Weeks and Mr. Beckett too. Roman's a fighter, you know."

"I can't believe they're actually going to be our neighbors," Mary Grace said. "What will Mama say?"

"Who is this we're talking about?" Herschel asked.

"Oh, I *am* sorry," Mary Grace said, her voice like honey again. "Just a casual acquaintance; a brother of one of the girls in LaVonda's class at school. Do you think we could get some music, Herschel?"

Herschel was glad to oblige. After some fiddling with the dial he settled for "Rhythms from the Ballroom of the Royal Hotel." It was a lovely night. The breeze had cooled us off, the music was the dreamy kind you don't really have to listen to, and the three dips of ice cream had left me comfortably full.

Herschel said, "Look at that moon, Mary Grace." They were on a first name basis, I noticed. "I think it's trying to follow you."

Well, I thought to myself, they really deserve each other.

CHAPTER
4

"If I had the wings of an an-gel; Over these prison walls I would fly." The first thing I heard next morning was Mrs. Budd's singing. I took the stairs two at a time and found her at the kitchen sink slapping china from dishpan to drainer.

"LaVonda, dearie, what's it going to be?" She gestured broadly as she spoke, and peaks of soapsuds slithered to the floor. "I told your mama I'd man the kitchen this morning. While I'm here, I do intend to pull my own weight." She looked down at herself and laughed. "And that's considerable."

"You're not fat," I protested. "You're just round."

"Vonnie!" My mother was appalled. "What a thing to say."

"Well, I'm not your Marlene Dietrich." Mrs. Budd leaned back against the sink, sucked her cheeks in, and half-closed her eyes. Mama smiled briefly and I giggled, but Mrs. Budd laughed until the tears came. As she was drying her eyes on the dish towel, I noticed the look of horror on Mama's face. Mrs. Budd noticed too and ordered her to her room. "Put your feet up, Edna," she said. "Fan yourself."

"Perhaps I will," Mama said vaguely. "Let me get you a fresh dish towel first."

"What's the matter with Mrs. Mercer?" Roxanne had just passed Mama in the doorway. "She looked sputtery and red in the face."

"Nothing to worry about," Mrs. Budd said. She was clattering through Mama's neatly stacked pans trying to find a skillet. "I think she just had a hot flash. What do you girls want for breakfast? A fried egg sandwich with catsup?"

Just then Pidd came sneaking around the doorjamb and shot Mrs. Budd with his Buck Rogers disintegrator gun. She shot him back with the egg turner, and Fred rushed in from the porch, barking at first one and then the other. Fred was old and grumpy and forever demanding peace. I understood his feelings, but I personally felt that this was the most interesting breakfast I'd ever had.

"Hey, Vonnie, we may have something important here." Roxanne unfolded a square of limp, smudged paper and read aloud, "6-30-26-10; 30-44-10-36. What's that? The combination to your safe?"

She handed it to me and I saw immediately that it was one of the secret messages Pidd and Chuffy taped under the porch swing. "I think that's Orphan Annie's Radio Code," I told her. With a stub of pencil from my pocket, I drew an alphabet grid, studied it a minute, and handed back the note. "It says 'Come over.'"

Roxanne was disgusted. "Is that all?"

I shrugged and stretched out on the glider again. We'd been trying to decide how to spend our first day together. Roxanne had remembered that the Grand changed Coming Attractions on Saturday; if you were there at the right time, you could get the old posters. We had half a mind to go down and pick up Ronald Colman.

"With all this good material right under his nose,

he writes a note like that?'' She shook her head. ''That's stupid.''

I explained to her that except for codes, Pidd wasn't really stupid. He could take a cornstalk and make a violin that really played, he could make whistles out of hickory bark, and by pushing the pith out of an elder shoot, he could fashion a fairly dangerous pop gun. ''But what do you mean by 'all this good material'?'' I asked.

''Well, if I were still young enough to play cops and robbers I'd be more practical. I'd do something meaningful.'' The porch swing creaked back and forth while she thought about it. ''I'd watch your grandfather, for one. He has his own private entrance, doesn't he? I'd see who came to see him and when and for how long. And Mrs. Fingerle. Nobody knows much about her. She doesn't have any friends in Elk Run. Why not? What's she trying to hide?''

I shook my head. I didn't know of anything offhand.

''And your sister. Pidd could chart her boyfriends. Find out which one has the edge.''

''I don't think Mary Grace would allow that.'' I couldn't see her letting Pidd within a hundred yards of one of her young men.

"Really, Vonnie. You don't ask permission to spy on people."

"But why would you—or Pidd, rather—want to spy on anybody in the first place?"

"It's educational. Remember when we had the poetry unit and Miss Piper said we should be observant? If you don't mind my saying so, Vonnie, you could be a heck of a lot more observant. You win prizes, you know facts, but you don't know people." She tapped my arm for emphasis. "You've got to understand what makes people tick."

"I guess that's important, isn't it?" I was watching the cedar waxwings in the ornamental mulberry just beyond the porch. About a dozen of them, lined up on a branch, had politely passed a berry from one bird to the next, right down the line.

"Sure it is, especially if you're a girl." She leaned back in the swing, eyes closed, arms behind her head. "It's the only way I know how to operate."

I noticed that her chest was bigger than Mary Grace's. If I'd looked like that, I would have worn a big floppy shirt, but Roxanne had on a tight yellow satin blouse with long darts pointing straight up.

She caught me staring at her and smiled at me through half-closed eyes. "Don't worry," she said. "You'll grow. I used to worry all the time, and now look at me."

"No," I said, louder than I'd meant to. Grandpa was working in his office with the window open so I lowered my voice. "What I mean is, I don't care about growing."

"Sure you do." Roxanne laughed tolerantly. "Boys like girls with good builds."

"If that's the case," I told her, "I'd just as soon shrink."

Perhaps we *had* disturbed Grandpa. At any rate, he came whistling around the corner of the porch. "LaVonda, I'm two stamps short. This is my morning for writing angry letters to the editors—one of the small pleasures of being retired—but *sic transit gloria;* no stamps." He gave my braid a little tug and patted me on the back; Grandpa was always happy when he was writing angry letters. "Would you go to the post office for me?"

"Yes sir. We were going downtown anyway to get *The Prisoner of Zenda* poster."

"Ah yes," Grandpa said. "Hentzau, an engaging rogue. That's the young Fairbanks, isn't it?"

"Yes sir. But Roxanne wants Ronald Colman. He plays Rudolf Rassendyll."

Grandpa handed me a nickel and a penny for the stamps and began to search the depths of his old leather purse. "I want to find a nickel for you and one for your friend for ice cream."

"Gee, it's a long way to the post office," Roxanne said. "And it's really warming up out there."

My mouth dropped open. I mean, it wasn't every day that I got a nickel to spend, and I didn't think Roxanne was any better off. Then it occurred to me that maybe she was angling for a dime.

It must have occurred to Grandpa, too, because he fixed her with his level, unblinking principal's stare. "Do you remember your Aesop?" he asked her.

She hemmed and hawed.

"You might do well to reread 'The Dog and the Bone,'" he said, handing me Roxanne's nickel as well as my own.

"Oh, I'll go with her," she said, in an offhand manner. "I don't really mind."

We took our time getting to town. People were out picking up limbs or staking flowers and nearly everybody had a word or two about the storm. Several times Pidd and Chuffy zoomed around us with their hoops, bouncing them off the curb and flipping them back on again without a wobble. We traded insults with them until they were out of sight. Then we had to sidestep a couple of hopscotch games and settle an argument about whether the rock was on a line or not. And in the block where the sidewalk wasn't made, there was a marble game in progress.

The stakes were high—a hundred in the ring—so we watched that for a while.

Even when we got to town, we didn't hurry. We pretended to spend our money in different ways, which gave us an excuse to look in all the store windows. We could have bought two sacks of tobacco at the grocery store—Roxanne was tempted momentarily—or shared an order of franks and kraut at Pete's or had a shave at the Elk Run Barber Shop. We could have also bought *Flash Gordon* with Evil Ming on the cover but, since we'd read most of it while we were in the drug store anyway, we settled for a double-decker fudge ripple.

"You've got a good deal," Roxanne said after we'd bought the stamps.

"What do you mean?"

"Well, you've got a two-story house with an attic and a cellar and lots of rooms. How many rooms you got, anyway?"

"I don't know," I told her. "I never counted."

"Are you rich?" Roxanne asked.

I looked at her in amazement. "Good heavens, no, we're not rich. We were in the Depression. Mama says we'll never get over it."

"Well, I think you're rich, no matter what you say." She looked at me critically, "You've got your own room, haven't you?"

"You've got it all wrong, Roxanne." I thought for a moment until I came up with the perfect example. "Mrs. Fingerle. She's got a Deusenberg. That's rich."

"There's something fishy about Mrs. Fingerle." Roxanne was back to that again. "I asked Mama why a lady like that would keep to herself, and Ma said she'd probably had bad luck with men."

"Mrs. Fingerle's okay," I told her. "She promised to teach me how to play cribbage. You want to learn?"

"Nope. Poker's my game. Do you play poker?"

I admitted that I didn't and Roxanne promised to show me how.

I told her that I really liked having a best friend to go around with, and she said she liked it, too. "At school," she said, "I used to think you were stuck up."

"That's amazing," I told her. "I thought the same thing about you."

The first thing I heard when I got back to the house was Mrs. Budd singing again. "My mother was a lady; like yours, you will allow."

"Who's sick?" I asked Mama as I passed her in the hall. She was carrying the tray we ate from when we were contagious. It was laid with a cutwork cloth and Grandma's china from Bavaria. There was also a miniature sweetheart rose with a spray of asparagus fern in a crystal vase.

"Nobody. Mrs. Fingerle asked for a tray in her room. She wants to rest."

"It looks pretty," I told her.

Mama smiled with sudden pleasure. "Thank you for noticing, Vonnie." Then she grew serious, all too soon. "I'll need you to help late this afternoon. Everybody will be in for supper."

"But Mrs. Budd is helping, isn't she?"

"I need *you*, Vonnie."

Pidd and Chuffy were trading Tarzan yells right outside the window—Mama steeled herself and gritted her teeth—and Mrs. Budd was finishing her song. "You wouldn't dare insult me, sir, if Jack were only here."

"Where's Mary Grace?" I asked. I could see my afternoon with Roxanne dwindling away.

"She rode into Whitehall with Herschel. He has to attend to some insurance matters."

"Edna?" Mrs. Budd was calling from the dining room. There was a tinkling of glass as the china cabinet door flew open. "Which glasses do you want me to use?" There was more clinking and jangling.

"I've got to go," Mama said to no one in particular and took off in a fast clip for the dining room.

I played poker with Roxanne all afternoon, but just when I was getting the hang of Baseball—treys and nines wild with a four-spot down for an extra card—I had to go help with supper. When I came into the kitchen, I noticed that Mama had straightened up at the sink and was rubbing the small of her back with her fist.

"Mama," I asked, "Will you have to do this every day?" I gestured to the potatoes which were about to boil over.

She made a dive for them. "Not every night, Vonnie." She thought for a moment. "We'll have a cold supper tomorrow night; it's Sunday."

"Why doesn't Sadie help you? She said she'd do anything at all." I was slicing oranges for ambrosia, being very careful to get the seeds out. I felt I needed to atone for not wanting to help.

"Mrs. Budd," Mama corrected. "I sent her to the garden to work."

"But isn't it too wet to chop weeds? Won't the ground pack?"

"Perhaps." Mama said the word as if she didn't care one way or the other. She gave me the core from the cabbage.

"You don't mind having company, do you, Mama?"

"Of course not. We have to do what we can to help."

"That's what Daddy and Grandpa say, but I just happened to think that they're not the ones who have to do the cooking."

I had never thought before that Mama minded working around the house. In fact, I thought she probably liked taking care of us. Now it occurred to me that maybe she hated housework as much as I hated homework. The idea that she was stuck with us made me uncomfortable.

"What would you do," I asked, "if you weren't a mother?"

"Why Vonnie, I couldn't think of not being a mother. I wouldn't want my life any other way."

"Didn't you want to go to college? Grandpa is always telling me I have to go. Didn't he tell you that?"

"Yes he did, Vonnie. He wanted his kind of life for me." She stared out the window, a knife in one hand, a green pepper in the other. "But what I wanted to do," she said with sudden force, "was marry your father." She looked back at me and laughed. "And I've never been sorry."

I chewed on my cabbage core and Mama went back to the cole slaw, but later, when she was rinsing the grater under the tap, she brought up the subject of education again. "Listen Vonnie, your grandfather is starting in early with you. You're a bright girl and you probably will want to go on with your studies. But don't let Grandpa persuade you to go to college, if you don't really want to. And don't let some young man influence you *not* to go. You do what *you* want."

I suppose I must have looked confused. She came over to me and gave me a little hug. "I just want my girls to be strong," she said. "I want Mary Grace to do what she wants, and you to do what you want."

"What about Pidd?"

"Pidd's a boy. Things will fall into place easier for him."

Supper was lively. Herschel and Mary Grace were full of talk about their trip to the city. "You wouldn't believe the ticket line for Benny Goodman. It was four blocks long!" Grandpa and Mrs. Fingerle discussed places from literature—Stratford on Avon, the Lake District, and Old Vic—and Mrs. Fingerle offered to put Grandpa in touch with her travel agent. "Now that you're retired, Everett, there's no reason you couldn't pop right over." (There was a reason, all right, but I knew Grandpa wouldn't mention it; talking about money or the lack of it was considered bad form.) Instead, he said that he was tempted, but "the political situation in Europe is so uncertain. One hesitates." Daddy had been working at the Bottoms all day and was able to answer Mrs. Budd's questions about her friends. "Joy and Buddy Warren have turned up. The morning of the storm they took a sudden notion to go to the New York World's Fair, of all places. They got as far as Cincinnati before they got homesick and made a U-turn with that pickup of theirs, right in the middle of Highway 42."

Halfway through the meal, the conversation turned to sports. After deciding that it would be Cincinnati and New York in the World Series, Daddy and the rest of the adults replayed the '38 game when Gabby Hartnett clinched the pennant for the Pirates with a home run in the dark. "Two outs in the bottom of the ninth," Mrs. Budd marvelled.

Pidd and I didn't say anything—we'd been taught not to interrupt adults—and Roxanne was too busy to talk. I had always thought Pidd was a pig, but Roxanne's speed with the fork was something to behold. Mrs. Fingerle, on the other hand, ate hardly anything. She took teaspoon servings and moved the food around on her plate, but I wasn't fooled. Mama kept pressing her, "Won't you try a bit of the chowchow; I make it myself and Matthew thinks it's tasty," or "This sauce is from our own apples."

Mrs. Fingerle politely declined.

Mary Grace and I had removed the plates and Mama was serving the ambrosia when the doorbell rang. Daddy answered and came back with Roman who stood in the doorway, glaring at us all. "I didn't want to come in," he said. "I only wanted to speak to Ma for a minute." He may have wanted to speak to Mrs. Budd, but the one he wanted to look at was evidently Mary Grace.

Mama looked startled but quickly recovered. "Sit down, Roman, and have dessert with us. I won't take no for an answer." Already she was making a place for him between me and Pidd. Mama's people came from the Deep South. I think if the Devil had dropped by, Mama would have felt duty-bound to make him a cup of tea.

Roman acknowledged introductions to the Fingerles and then sat stiffly, taking very small bites and admiring Mary Grace, until Daddy began to talk about the house Roman was building. Roman said he'd be ready to pour the basement next Wednesday if Daddy could arrange for the trucks.

"You'll never get it ready by that time, boy."

Roman just smiled.

"Where are you building?" Mama asked. She'd been watching Roman watching Mary Grace. All this staring was really kind of embarrassing. Mary Grace was as red as a beet, Herschel was confused, and Mama was suspicious.

Roman dragged his eyes away from Mary Grace and told Mama what most of us already knew. "On the Beckett place. On the rise above the little creek."

I saw her hand tighten on the cake knife, but all she said was, "What a pretty site for a house. Will you have a piece of cake?"

During a lull in the conversation, Grandpa told Roman that he'd heard he was working with Ed Weeks.

"That's right. I'm going to the University this fall. I'll get a degree in law."

"Well, well." My grandfather leaned back in his chair and looked on Roman approvingly. "That's quite an undertaking."

Roman must have thought that Grandpa meant that a law degree was quite an undertaking *for a Budd*. He got all touchy, the same way he did with me over the apples the day of the storm. He spoke curtly. "Mr. Weeks has arranged a scholarship. I have a job—night work—waiting for me. I'll do what has to be done."

"I'm sure you will," Grandpa said. "I have some books that might interest you. Blackstone, some readings in civil law. I'd like you to come round to the study some time."

"I'll be busy this summer. I want to get Roxanne and Ma settled into the new house before I leave. But I'll try."

Roman made it sound as if he'd be doing Grandpa a favor.

I don't think Roman meant to be uppity. I think his mother had probably never taught him all the "pleases" and "thank-yous" and all the little dishonesties we Mercers had to learn, like saying you had a nice time when you really didn't, or saying you didn't want another piece of cake when you really did.

Or like saying what Mama was saying now to Mrs. Budd: "Vonnie and Mary Grace will be glad to help me with the dishes. They're used to it and they don't mind a bit. I know they'd rather you go along and talk to Roman."

In the privacy of the kitchen, Mama and Mary Grace had several whispered, heated exchanges. Mary Grace said she couldn't help it if Roman stared at her, could she? Mama said that Mary Grace did seem to know him quite well, and Mary Grace said she'd never had a date with Roman in her life, but why shouldn't she? Mama said the Budds were . . . well, different.

"You mean they aren't as good as we are?" Mary Grace was slinging dishes right and left.

Mama said she didn't say that. "I said different."

Mrs. Budd, who'd been seated at the piano idly playing chords while she talked with Roman, turned round on the stool to face us. My dad put down the evening paper. "Play us a tune, Sadie," he said.

"Oh, do you play?" Mama asked politely. She had tried to interest both Mary Grace and me in the piano. Mary Grace took enough lessons from Miss Crutcher so she could play in the recital and wear a ruffly dress. I stopped taking so I wouldn't have to.

"Does she play!" my dad said, with unaccustomed enthusiasm. "Sadie, play 'Twelfth Street Rag' for them."

Sadie laughed and snapped her fingers. "That's right. You always liked 'Twelfth Street Rag,' Matthew."

"Yes, please play for us," Mama said in a tight little voice.

Sadie ran up and down the keys for a few times and then dived into the song. She played it in regular ragtime first, then in double time, which was so fast that her plump arms jiggled and the trinkets on top of the piano began to clink. My dad beamed and Pidd and I began to clap to the music and Grandpa moved his chair right up to the piano so he could watch Mrs.

Budd's fingers flying up and down the keyboard. She went right into "Nola" and then "The Doll Dance." We began to shout requests to her and there were none she couldn't honor, from one of the top ten on *Your Hit Parade*—"Bei Mir Bist du Schön"—to Grandpa's number "When the Moon Comes Over the Mountain." She played war songs for my dad, which he and my Grandpa sang, even harmonized to. This surprised me; I never knew they could sing. In church, Daddy usually dozed and Grandpa only mouthed the words, having been angry since the choir leader ordered new hymnals with songs "which only the Mormon Tabernacle Choir could sing." Now he was booming out the bass part on "Tipperary" and making up the words he didn't know to "Hinky-Dinky-Parlez-Vous."

But when Mary Grace sang, Grandpa and Daddy— everybody—stopped. It occurred to me that if Mary Grace would sing all the time, I wouldn't have a single complaint against her. Her voice was clear and sweet, so sweet it made me shiver. It was a magical sound, and listening to it made me believe in frogs turning into princes and animals talking on Christmas Eve. And watching her made me believe in fairy godmothers. There seemed to be a royal distance between Mary Grace and the rest of us, as if we were an audience of strangers. She held herself like a queen—her neck was slim and elegant, her smile was professionally cool. Roman and Herschel watched her intently, a situation which would have left me paralyzed, but seemed to encourage Mary Grace to sing even better than usual. There was a smugness about Roman's approval. I figured he was saying to himself, *Of course she can sing; she's the best.* But Herschel was as spellbound as I was. He just stood there, dumb struck and helpless.

Mary Grace retired in triumph, her cheeks prettily flushed, and refused to sing another note. "Quit while you're ahead," Roxanne whispered to me out of the corner of her mouth.

Mama, who had kept to her embroidery while the rest of us crowded around the piano now made a request. "Do you play classical, Mrs. Budd? I've always favored 'Für Elise.'" Her eyes dropped back down to the embroidery hoops while she clipped a thread.

Mrs. Budd chuckled. "Ah yes. You can't graduate from Miss Crutcher until you've mastered that little number." She proceeded to play those phrases that we'd faltered over so many times, counting our one-and-two-and-threes; but now we were hearing Beethoven, not an exercise marked: *Thursday—Watch Fingering.* While she played we all became quiet, melancholy even. Herschel stared at Mary Grace with soulful eyes; Roman stared into space as if he were reordering the universe.

When she finished, we were quiet for a moment; then all of us clapped. Mrs. Budd had provided us with a truly memorable evening.

"Well, that takes me back a few years," she said, closing the keyboard.

"I didn't know you were one of Miss Crutcher's pupils," Mama said.

"I suppose I was one of her first. My Ma traded ironing for music lessons." Mrs. Budd thought back over the years and shook her head. "That represents a lot of scales and a lot of washdays."

"I'm sure that if your Ma could've heard you tonight," my dad said, "she'd thought it worth her work. You play fine, Sadie, real fine."

"Go on with you, Matt," Sadie was her jolly self again. "How would you know? You've got a tin ear."

She and Roxanne said their good-nights and went up to their room. Mrs. Fingerle left shortly afterwards humming "Du, Du, Liegst Mir In Herzen," which Mrs. Budd had played for her. For the first time since her arrival, Mrs. Fingerle looked happy and relaxed.

I was already into my pajamas before I remembered my book, which I'd tucked behind the sofa pillows. I liked to read before I went to sleep, although Mama and Daddy didn't approve. But if I pushed the scatter rug against the crack under the door, no one would be the wiser, and I could finish the last few chapters of *Captain Blood*.

I padded down the stairs and stopped outside the living room. Mama and Daddy seemed to be having a serious discussion and I was undecided about interrupting. Mama was saying, "How did you know Mrs. Budd played the piano?"

"Everybody knows she plays the piano. She played at Jake's Place for years."

"Not everybody," Mama said. "I didn't know. But then I've never been to Jake's."

The news was droning away in the background—something about the Germans taking over some country or other—but Mama raised her voice and talked above it. "How did she know that you liked 'Twelfth Street Rag'?"

Daddy must have gotten interested in the news because Mama had to repeat the question. Finally he said, "Because I've asked her to play it on several occasions."

"Where? Where did you ask her to play it?"

"What *is* this, Edna? Twenty Questions?"

My mother didn't answer and finally my dad said,

"All right. On Fridays when I paid the help at the Yards, we sometimes knocked off early and went out to Jake's. The boys had a beer, listened to Sadie, and then went home. It was perfectly harmless."

"Then why did I have to find out about it from a perfect stranger?" Mama seemed close to tears.

"Because you would have made a fuss over nothing. I like to have a bit of fun, Edna—like we had tonight—and there's damn little of it around here."

"Matthew!" I knew Mama was objecting to the word "damn."

"That's exactly what I mean. It's 'Matthew, watch your language' or 'Matthew, remember the children' or 'Matthew, don't upset Father' or 'Matthew, we can't afford it.'"

I knew as soon as he said it that Daddy shouldn't have mentioned money, and sure enough, Mama's next words were clipped and hard. "Well, somebody around here better watch the nickels and dimes."

"The Depression is over, Edna. We can go to a movie. We can eat in a restaurant." Daddy was emphasizing his words like a schoolteacher making points. "We could even take a little trip this summer. Would you like that, Edna?"

"It will never be over for me," Mama said. I'd never heard her talk so mean. "I will save every penny I can get my hands on, because I don't intend to go through that again."

After a while, my dad said very quietly, "I was there too, remember?"

Mama didn't answer.

Daddy must have gone back to his newspaper; I heard rustling. "Don't save too much," he said after a while. "You have to spend some things while you have the chance."

I couldn't believe my parents were talking like this. They were my Mama and Daddy, and they weren't supposed to be arguing like Pidd and me or Mary Grace and me. They could fuss at us all they wanted—we expected it—but not at each other.

I tiptoed back upstairs without my book. I couldn't have read anyway. My insides were churning and I thought I might lose my supper.

CHAPTER
5

Our summer had begun to seem like one long celebration. Although it was well into July and the days were long and hot, it was Christmas in the kitchen. With Mary Grace's help Mama turned out cakes and pies and dozens of buns, and the air was sweet with cinnamon and yeast. In fact, with company about, the most ordinary activities seemed to take on a holiday flavor. In the late mornings when it was still shady on the side porch, we snapped beans or shelled limas, but with the gossip flying as fast as our fingers, it really didn't seem like work. Even Mrs. Fingerle joined us, sitting regally in the peacock chair, carefully examining each leaf of chard or peering suspiciously into the butter bean pods. The garden was lush, productive beyond Mama's wildest dreams, and day after day we scrubbed new potatoes and shucked sweet corn or peeled June apples, which were never ripe until July. Even with the company Mama found time to can. The big kettle bubbled on the back burner, the air in the kitchen was close and steamy, and the windows seemed to wear a perpetual coat of mist.

One morning while we were slicing cucumbers for bread-and-butter pickles, Pidd brought the mail to the porch with a letter for Mrs. Fingerle on top. Conversation stopped while she read it.

I suppose everybody is curious about letters. My first impulse was to ask, "Well, who's it from? What's it all about?" But, of course, none of us asked Mrs. Fingerle. With shaking hands, she shoved the letter into her pocket and rose from her chair. The newspaper she'd held in her lap and all of the long green slivers of cucumber peel slid to the floor. "Excuse me," she said, not looking at any of us or bothering about the peels. "I think I shall lie down for a moment."

"Shall I get you a headache powder?" Mama asked.

"No, no. I'm quite all right. I merely want to rest." She hurried into the house, leaving our unasked questions unanswered.

"I don't know what to make of that," Mrs. Budd announced. "She seemed fine as frog hair when we first came out."

"I think there must have been unsettling news in that letter," Mama said.

"But she said she was quite all right, didn't she?" I saw that Mrs. Budd was slicing the cucumbers much too thick to suit Mama. She liked them wafer thin, not chunky.

"Some people are reticent about sharing problems with strangers, Mrs. Budd." Mama spoke more sharply than usual, but then everything about Mama was sharper than usual. In the past several weeks her frown lines had deepened, her mouth had set into a hard crease, her movements had become short and choppy.

Mrs. Budd seemed not to notice the sharpness. "People ought to share their problems," she said genially. "It's bad to keep things bottled up."

Roxanne raised an eyebrow and gestured toward the creek. I knew she'd want to talk about the letter as soon as we could get away, which was no problem for her; she simply walked off. But I still had to fetch and carry, which was my mission in life. Mary Grace and Mama worked as a team in the kitchen, Mary Grace anticipating Mama's orders to sift that or grease the other. She knew when icing spun a thin thread and when egg whites came to a soft peak. I didn't, so I got picked for the menial chores like bringing up jars from the cellar, going after onions from the garden, or rounding up the pickling spices. But eventually, having done my stint inside, I delivered the cucumber peels to the compost and kept right on going toward the creek.

Roxanne was sitting on Pidd's boards having her cigarette. She allowed herself only one a day because she didn't want to get into the habit. I must say she smoked elegantly, with her forefinger on the top of the cigarette, her thumb on the bottom, and the other three fingers extended. Without any kind of greeting, she asked me right off, "What was in the letter? You were closest. Did you see?"

I shook my head.

Roxanne was exasperated. "You could have tried, Vonnie. You have to make an effort to find out things. You can't wait for information to fall in your lap."

I made an effort. "As I remember"—I tried to visualize the address—"the penmanship was not the greatest. Probably some little kid wrote it."

"Or else the poor writing was a disguise. Maybe the letter was really from her lover."

"Roxanne!"

"Oh, I know she's too old now. I mean a former lover."

"No, Roxanne; you've got it all wrong. People in Elk Run don't have lovers, for goodness' sake."

She took a last, long drag from her cigarette and flipped it out over the water. "Okay then," she said, exhaling smoke. "How do you explain Herschel?"

"Herschel is Mrs. Fingerle's nephew."

"Who says?"

"Mrs. Fingerle says, that's who."

Roxanne smiled knowingly. "I see. Mrs. Fingerle says."

"Everybody says."

"And where's *Mr.* Fingerle?" she asked. She picked up a pebble and casually sailed it down the creek. It skipped five times.

"He's dead, I guess."

"But you don't really know, do you?"

"If you have to have proof, Roxanne, go to the cemetery." I stood up, brushed off my shorts, and started toward the house. Roxanne ran after me.

"Good idea," she said. "I do have to have proof. I can't accept 'what everybody says' like you do. I know for a fact—my aunt used to work for the

Fingerles in the old days—that Mrs. Fingerle went away on a trip." Even though there wasn't a soul in sight, Roxanne began to whisper. "She was supposed to have been in Europe for five months. Then one day she comes back with a baby and a string of baby nurses."

"So what?"

"Well, if one of the girls from the Bottoms went away for five months and came home with a baby, believe me, nobody would assume she'd just become an aunt." She hooted merrily and nudged me in the ribs.

I hadn't been serious about going to the cemetery, but I didn't mind even though we had to go to the opposite side of town to get there. I liked to see who was around, maybe have a few words with them. But Roxanne wasn't too thrilled when I talked to people. If I came to a complete stop, she'd cloud up and stalk on ahead. (She wasn't interested in all people, I decided; just those who were close to her.) Homer Henry, at the hardware store, was lettering his name on the new plate glass window he'd put in after the storm. We had to talk about how bad the high water was for fishing. (Roxanne tapped her foot impatiently.) Mrs. Morsey was out considering her new front porch. She thought the raw yellow lumber looked just plain tacky against the weathered brick and the ivy vines and she was tired of waiting for the painters; she had a good notion to paint it herself. (Roxanne whistled through her teeth while we talked.) The four big maples down by the post office had been sawed to stumps, having been split by the storm, and Miss Nettie, the postmistress, was setting out geraniums around them. "A small memorial," she said. (Roxanne studied her nails.)

A truck rumbled by then with a load of lumber sticking out the back. My dad recognized the two of us and backed to a stop. "Are you ladies going my way?" he asked.

I told him we were going to the cemetery.

"I guess that's where we're all going," he laughed. "Hop in."

I was happy to see him and glad to be sitting next to him. Lately he was working so hard that he seldom came home for lunch, and sometimes we even ate supper without him. On those occasions, Mama kept his food warm in the oven and he ate by himself in the kitchen. I never heard the two of them fussing after that one night. In fact, they were extremely polite to each other when they talked, which wasn't too often.

I missed not having him around. For one thing, he could fix anything. If we wanted a kite made, a shelf put up, or a necklace repaired, it was my dad we went to. And afterward, he might scoop us up and hoist us into the air—Mary Grace, too. And even while we were suspended, we could look down on those broad shoulders and thick neck and know that trouble wasn't going to get too close to us with our daddy staring it in the eye. But with him not around so much, the members of our household acted like the kids on the playground before the teacher came out and blew the whistle. Everybody was running around in different directions, bumping into one another, not getting anywhere.

"Roxanne?" My dad had to shout over the rattle of the lumber and the roar of the motor. "Have you seen your house lately? Roman's moving right along with it. You might be moved in this time next month."

"I haven't seen it this week," Roxanne shouted back.

The truck rolled to a stop at the wrought iron arch that stood at the cemetery entrance. "I've got a delivery for Roman," Daddy said. "Tell you what; I'll pick you up in half an hour. You can ride along with me if you want." We said "okay" and the truck rattled away, its red flags bouncing.

I started angling up the rise toward the Fingerle plot. I knew my way around. Pidd and I used to come gather persimmons from a tree at the very back of the graveyard, and we also came for hickory nuts in the fall. Then once a year all our family—the aunts, uncles, and cousins—got together to clean up the Mercer–Comstock plots. We trimmed the roses back and cut grass and raked, and then we had a covered-dish picnic on the church grounds. I was explaining to Roxanne about the picnic when all of a sudden I realized she wasn't following me. I looked back and there she was, still standing where my dad had left us. She looked strange.

"What's the matter?" I called back. "Did you get sick bouncing around in the truck?"

"I don't think it's such a good idea to look up Mr. Fingerle's grave," she said. I could see now that her eyes were glassy.

"I never did," I told her. "But since we're here, we might as well have a look."

"You look if you want to. I'll wait."

I looked at her carefully. "Roxanne, are you sure you aren't sick? You're white as a ghost." As soon as I said the word "ghost," I remembered the silly superstitions about graveyards, and I realized that Roxanne was actually scared.

"Do you know," she said solemnly, "that if you step on a grave your days are numbered?"

"That's ridiculous. How could you pull grass from around a headstone if you didn't step on the grave?"

"It's true." she said. "Bobby Dan Pinkston came

out here on a dare last Halloween. He stood on old lady Yates' grave, and the very next day he was dead."

"Well really, Roxanne, he was killed in a car accident. He was going ninety miles an hour, drunk as a lord. You can't blame that on Mrs. Yates."

"But it did happen," she said. "If you want to go plowing around a graveyard you're more than welcome to. I intend to sit right here and wait for your dad." With hands on her hips, she looked at me as if I were a little child who had to be humored. "Better be careful not to get overheated, though. You could have sunstroke, you know."

I was so astounded I couldn't speak. How could things have turned themselves around so? I took off running and, knowing that she was watching me, I deliberately stepped on Aunt Maybelle Mercer's grave, rest her soul.

By the time I had reached the far corner of the cemetery and dropped down under the big old cedar tree in the fence row, I felt much better. I was out of Roxanne's sight and up the hill far enough to catch a breeze. There was no sound except from the bees hovering around the honeysuckle and a mockingbird who was perched atop the highest Fingerle monument, singing his heart out. I sat for some time, enjoying my solitude. As much fun as it was having company and a best friend, I did miss those times when I'd gone off to the creek to think, all by myself. Roxanne was always with me now, and she always wanted to do things and go places—except to cemeteries, that is.

A car door slammed. With a flash of white tail, the bird flew off and I decided I'd better locate Mr. Fingerle before my dad returned. I was poking around the Fingerle–Gruber plot, checking names and dates, when the Johnson girls came ambling through the monuments. They weren't really girls, being even older than Grandpa, but everybody called them girls because they'd never married.

"Lovely, isn't it?" Miss Frances looked with me at Mrs. Fingerle's stone, a tall monolith of marble inscribed: *Marta Gruber Fingerle; Born 1873–*

"So comforting to have one's stone waiting for one," Miss Hattie said. Personally, although I wasn't superstitious about cemeteries, I didn't think I'd appreciate having a stone and a dash waiting for me each time I visited.

"Well, sister," Miss Frances said, "shall we unload the car?"

I helped them set out the fluted tin baskets filled with orange blossoms that smelled heavenly, big floppy pink peonies and Dutch irises and sprays of gladioli. I told them that I didn't think a florist could make prettier arrangements.

"Well, thank you dear. You know we always cut early in the mornings. Then we let the flowers soak in water until after lunch. (We have early lunch on cemetery days.) Then we do the arrangements. I think the soaking is the secret, don't you, Frances?"

While they discussed the question I looked behind, in front, and to both sides of Mrs. Fingerle's monument, but I couldn't find her husband. It occurred to me that if anybody would know about his resting place, the Johnson girls would. They knew more about dead people than anybody in town.

"About Herschel Fingerle," I began. "His father . . ."

Miss Frances grabbed my arm with little bird claws and began to think out loud. "Let's see now," she said. "Herschel would be Fred's son. Isn't that right, sister?"

"Yes," Miss Hattie answered, "I believe that's the way it was. Hans Kauffman had three boys and one girl—that was Hilda—and she married a Gruber, and they had the two girls, Marta and Frieda."

"And Frieda married Karl's son. Now whose grandson would that be?"

There was more genealogy which, like the "begats" in the Bible, I ignored. Finally, during a lull in the conversation when they were trying to determine which Fingerle went off to Ohio, I returned to the original subject. "Is Herschel really Mrs. Fingerle's nephew?" I asked.

Miss Frances dropped my arm like it had the plague. She looked at Miss Hattie and they both looked away from me. Finally, Miss Hattie said she was shocked that I'd asked such a question.

"A child of your age shouldn't be interested in such things," Miss Frances added. "What would your mother say?"

Daddy honked just then so I said my good-byes and the Johnsons sent their regards to my grandfather. I hadn't found Mr. Fingerle, and I had to admit that Roxanne knew more than I did after all.

When we drove into Roman's clearing the first person I saw was Mary Grace. That was a surprise! It was quite a trek from our place to the Becketts' and Mary Grace hated to walk. But there she was all decked out in the yellow embroidered eyelet she'd made for Senior Day. She was watching Roman, who was laying sheeting on the roof. He was working without a shirt and his bare brown back rippled with muscles and glistened with sweat. Although she hadn't shown much of an interest in roofing before, now she was so enraptured that she didn't hear the truck drive up. She nearly jumped out of her wits when I slammed the door.

"Mrs. Budd was going to bring over some water for Roman," she said. "I told her I'd come instead. She wanted to listen to 'Backstage Wife' and 'Stella Dallas.' Mama's gone to a meeting at the church. She couldn't get out of it."

She explained all of this in one breath, and I looked at her in amazement. Heavens, I didn't care about Mrs. Budd and "Stella Dallas" or Mama's meeting at the church.

Roman came down the ladder like an acrobat from the top of the tent. He registered surprise at Mary Grace's presence but accepted the water eagerly. Not bothering with the glass she tried to hand him, he tipped the jar and drank heartily. When he finished with an "Ah, that was good," water still trickled down his chin. Mary Grace reached out her hand as though she were going to wipe it off. He smiled, and she blushed scarlet.

After he and my dad had unloaded and stacked the lumber, we all had a tour of the house. Planks had been laid across the floor joists, and we edged our way from room to room while Roman explained that "this would be Roxanne's room; she's never had a room to herself," and that the kitchen, dining room, and living room would be one large area because "all our friends gather in the kitchen, anyway." This was a new idea for me. Our company was parlor company and Mama set great store by always having one room in immaculate condition for receiving guests.

About that time two cars of Roman's friends from the Bottoms drove up with great whooping and laughing. "My work crew," Roman grinned. He watched while they carried a case of beer from one of the cars and a galvanized tub from the other. Two of the young men began to chink at a block of ice. "They work fairly well as long as the beer stays cold," Roman said. My dad grinned as if this were natural enough, but I could tell by Mary Grace's mouth that she was as shocked as I was. If Mama only knew what was going on so close to home . . .

All the time the young men were icing the beer, they examined Mary Grace. My dad was checking the studding and didn't notice, but Roman did. He strolled over to his friends, said a few words that I couldn't hear, and after that they seemed to go out of their way not to notice her.

They didn't pay any attention to me either, except for one boy who said in passing, "Hey, little girl, you still got those Huns living at your house?"

"Huns? What do you mean, Huns?"

"You know. That pair of Krauts."

Daddy called us then and said he'd give us a lift to the house if Roxanne and I didn't mind sitting in the back. Mary Grace sat in front with Daddy, of course. She would have died before she'd ridden in the truck bed. But I liked letting the wind whip my hair and waving to people and singing at the top of my lungs. I hoped I never got too old to ride in the back of the truck.

When we got to our house, we stopped so suddenly that Roxanne and I were hurled against each other. Daddy jumped out of the cab and ran to the gate. Roxanne and I leaned over the side of the truck and saw the sign. In broad daylight someone had tacked a big black swastika on our gate with big red splotches of blood dripping down. Daddy ripped it off and tossed it into the truck bed.

"Now listen," he said. "You're not to say anything about this. Do you understand? I don't want to worry anybody with this trash. Okay?"

I nodded. In our family we were always protecting people, keeping troublesome things from them. Sometimes I thought it might be better in the long run to tell everything right out, instead of sidestepping so much, but of course I had to do what Daddy said.

He pointed a finger at Roxanne, whose eyes were dancing with excitement. "And that means you, young lady."

Roxanne was not used to taking orders and she started to get huffy. My dad was not at all impressed. He glared and pointed his finger at her. "You do understand?"

Finally, just like Pidd or I would have done, she dropped her eyes and said, "Yes, sir."

"Guten Nachmittag, Frau Fingerle."

"Guten Nachmittag, Frāulein Mercer."

As usual, I deposited the tea tray in front of Mrs. Fingerle at four o'clock sharp. *"Danke,"* she'd say, and I would answer *"Bitte sehr"* and then having exhausted my German vocabulary, we would speak in English.

"Roxanne is not with you, I see." Mrs. Fingerle poured the tea and put in four lumps for me.

I shook my head. Roxanne seldom visited. At first, she came regularly because, according to her, it never did any harm to befriend the elderly. She'd read stories of old people popping off and leaving thousands of dollars to the paper boy, a nurse maybe, or the little girl who came to read to them in the afternoons. She'd paid outrageous compliments to Mrs. Fingerle and hinted for jewelry until I was embarrassed for her. None of it worked. Mrs. Fingerle told her to sit up straight, spit out her gum, and pronounce her final consonants.

Mrs. Fingerle passed me the nut bread. "I think I shall give her my coral necklace."

I was dumbfounded. I couldn't believe she'd been taken in by Roxanne's artless begging.

"That disturbs you," Mrs. Fingerle said with a half smile. "But you see, I don't need the necklace; Roxanne does. And she needs the giving of it. You do not know that kind of hunger."

"I suppose not." I still didn't understand. In our family, we'd been taught not to wheedle.

"Now," she said briskly. "Where shall we go today?"

Every afternoon Mrs. Fingerle told me about her travels. She told me about having tea in a country inn outside of Tokyo and about seeing the rescue dogs at the Hospice of St. Bernard. She described the Highland Games and Indian dances and terrible bullfights and boat races on the Thames. I was enthralled; I couldn't seem to get enough. "Tell me more," I kept saying. While she talked, I could close my eyes and almost believe I was floating in a gondola. I could taste the *croissants* and hear the bagpipes.

"I want to go everywhere and see everything," I told her. "I want to know all there is to know." Then I laughed, being a little ashamed of my outburst. "But of course, I never will."

"That's *your* hunger, LaVonda, and you're right; you never will know all there is to know. But what an exciting time you'll have learning what you can."

I had to laugh. "I've never even been to Louisville. I can't see myself getting to Lisbon."

"You'll go. Roxanne will be satisfied with baubles; it will take the world for you."

She sat quietly, tall and straight and uncompromising, busy with her own thoughts. I'd learned not to interrupt.

"I can arrange for you to have a part of it," she said, after a time. "I shall speak to your parents." She did not comment further, and at 4:45, as usual, I was dismissed.

Roxanne couldn't understand why I continued to take up the tea. "She's such a cold fish," she said.

It was true that Mrs. Fingerle wasn't affectionate, although I think she liked me; she no longer complained about the four lumps of sugar in my tea. And she certainly wasn't an easy woman to be around. I was expected to think before I spoke and to phrase my thoughts in the best possible way. On the other hand she considered what I said seriously, she answered my questions honestly, and she made me feel that I mattered.

"It's not that she's cold," I told Roxanne. "She just thinks responsibility is more important than love. She told me that all the sentimentality in the world mattered less than one person's seeing his duty and doing it."

"Well, I don't agree with that," Roxanne said. "From what I read in *Love Gems* and *Sweethearts Today*—I got both magazines this morning—love conquers all. That's all we need in this world, Vonnie." She popped another chocolate into her mouth.

"Plus a little nourishment," I said.

She giggled and passed me the box.

I guess we shouldn't have delved into the bottom layer. That night I couldn't get to sleep for thinking of swastikas and letters and cucumber peels and tombstones.

CHAPTER
6

In August the temperature rose and leveled at a hundred. The air was heavy with moisture; for days there'd been no rain and very little breeze. The shades and windows came down in the morning to trap the small coolness of the night, and the house stayed dark and hushed. The grass was parched—the sprinklers swished most of the day—and Fred, who'd dug back under the spirea bush, came out only for water. Inside, there was a constant whir of electric fans. Drawers stuck, bread molded, and tempers flared.

During the day, the ladies took long naps in darkened rooms or sat drinking pitchers of iced tea, scarcely making the effort to talk. They picked up their needlework, took a stitch or two, then laid it aside for long periods of time. The radio played constantly—Father Coughlin denounced Roosevelt, DiMaggio hit homers, H. V. Kaltenborn explained the news—but nobody cared, one way or the other.

Our oldest guest seemed especially listless, and Mama urged her to see a doctor. Mrs. Fingerle declined, insisting that it was "just this miserable heat." I wondered if she might not be worried about the letters. She had received another half dozen addressed in the same childish scrawl, whose contents she kept to herself. Roxanne had the idea that the whole lot had been entrusted to Grandpa, so perhaps he knew something we didn't. At any rate, Grandpa was making a point of bringing in the mail each day, and since he had, the letters to Mrs. Fingerle had stopped arriving. I think he'd also appointed himself her protector. He took her for drives in the evening and asked her to play chess with him and brought her books he thought she might enjoy.

Mrs. Budd noticed his attentions. She said to

Mama once, "Your father must have been lonely before Mrs. Fingerle came."

Mama laughed dryly. "Not in this household." (Mary Grace and some of her friends were arguing over whether or not it was too hot to play bridge.)

"Having young people around is not the same as having a friend your own age," Mrs. Budd insisted. "Somebody outside the family."

"Father is quite content."

"Nevertheless," Mrs. Budd laughed, "we'd better watch those two. Might have a romance going on right under our noses."

"How you do go on, Mrs. Budd."

After that, Mama watched Grandpa and Mrs. Fingerle all the time. She also began to be particularly concerned about Grandpa's comfort. "Father," she'd say, "Have this chair. It's more comfortable," or "Sit over here where you can get more of the fan."

Like the rest of us, Grandpa was snappish with the heat. "I'm not an invalid, Edna," he'd say.

Roxanne stayed inside all day crunching ice. She spent more and more time reading her detective stories and movie magazines, or helping her mother enter contests: I LIKE ROSEBUD BEAUTY BATH BECAUSE, *in twenty-five words or less.* She also worked on her chain letters, carefully copying names and addresses, and enclosing a dime with each. Ten recipients were supposed to put Roxanne's name on ten more letters, and someday soon she was supposed to get back twenty thousand dollars. She was doing the same with handkerchiefs. I wondered what a person would do with twenty thousand handkerchiefs.

Sometimes when Roxanne was busy with her correspondence, I went to see Roman. He didn't seem to mind the heat. His clothes were dark with sweat and he drank gallons of water, but he said he was too busy to pay attention to the thermometer. Early in the morning he drove Mr. Beckett's truck into Whitehall to deliver vegetables to the grocery stores. Then he worked for Mr. Weeks in the law office until two or three in the afternoon, when he began to work on his house.

I held the ends of boards while he sawed or handed him nails, and we talked. I asked him why he wanted to be a lawyer. It seemed to me that he was a pretty good housebuilder, so why didn't he stick to that?

"I don't want to be a lawyer, Vonnie; I *have* to be. I want to get into politics and it seems to me that law is the quickest route to the Statehouse."

"Why do you want to be in politics?"

We were stirring paint and for a while we plunged the stick deep into the can and lifted it through the paint, and then watched the stream of *Sunshine Yellow* flow back into the can again. "Mesmerizing," I said, and he nodded agreement.

Finally, he laid the paint paddle across the top of the can and leaned back against the crate containing Mrs. Budd's new kitchen sink. "Because I want to change things," he said. "That's why I'm going into politics. People have such short memories, Vonnie. The economy's on the upswing now; social reform will soon be a dead issue. But I intend to be around to remind people that we still have the poor, the elderly, and the blacks." He pointed to the Negro who was puttying around the window. "Do you know that Ned can't check a book out of the Elk Run Public Library?"

"Does Mrs. Fingerle know about it? She gave the land and the building to the town. I bet she'd change the rules."

"Vonnie, she *makes* the rules."

"Then I don't think she understands them," I insisted. "She's basically kind, Roman. Grandpa says she gives away scholarships and Christmas checks and statues for the parks. And most of the town depends on the Fingerle Mills; you know that."

"Sure it does," Roman said, "in the same way the survival of the slaves was dependent on the largesse of the plantation owners. The Fingerle family can afford to be paternalistic toward the workers, Vonnie. If it hadn't been for the union, they'd still be paying slave wages."

"Largesse?" I said.

He laughed. "If you can say mesmerizing, I can say largesse."

"One of Grandpa's words," I explained.

"How about that? A slip of a kid and a Budd from the Bottoms using five-dollar words."

He pried off the lid of a quart of semi-gloss *Sunshine Yellow*. "I have to be honest with you, Vonnie. There's another reason I want to get into politics, a personal reason." He pointed the paint paddle at me. "I am not about to be dismissed as a Budd from the Bottoms. Pop has run away all his life and Ma accepts whatever comes, but I intend to fight." He looked at me as if he were ready to begin battle on the spot. Then he grinned and pulled my pigtail. "Are you going to vote for me for governor, Vonnie?"

"I sure will," I said. "You're my only friend right now. Roxanne doesn't want to come out in the heat, Grandpa's busy taking care of Mrs. Fingerle, Daddy's gone all the time, Mama gets crosser and crosser, and Pidd's with Chuffy from daylight till dark."

"What about Mary Grace?" Roman asked.

"Who knows about Mary Grace? She's either

bubbling over with good cheer, or else she's walking around like a zombie. Up and down."

I didn't say so, but it seemed to me that when she was with Herschel, she was at the top of the seesaw. But when Roman appeared on the scene, she bumped to the bottom. She snapped at me and picked at her nail polish and stared moodily out the window for long periods of time. I remembered that she and Herschel were always talking when they were together. I asked Roman if he and Mary Grace ever talked.

"No, not like you and I do," he said. "I don't think your sister is interested in social reform."

"You're right there. I can't see her getting too excited over a campaign to let Ned use the library. I think she would hate it. She's always saying to me: 'Vonnie, don't make a spectacle of yourself.' She wouldn't like your making a spectacle of yourself, Roman."

"She doesn't have to get involved." There was a mystical look about him now, a secret smile that seemed to exclude me. He was also dripping paint all over, and I told him he'd better watch what he was doing.

"I don't see why you want to go around with somebody who's not interested in the same things you are," I said. "I mean, not even a little bit interested. And I sure don't understand liking somebody you can't even talk to."

"You will when you get older." He gave me that patronizing look that Roxanne and Mary Grace sometimes favored me with.

I got really mad at that. "You're just like everybody else," I snapped. "They're always saying *Why don't you grow up, Vonnie? Act like a young lady.* Then when I try to understand adults, when I ask questions, it's always *You're too young, Vonnie. Wait till you grow up.*"

Roman thought about that while I sulked. "You're right," he said after a while. "It's a difficult time for you. So I will tell you that your sister represents everything I've never had: grace, beauty, refinement, talent." He had listed Mary Grace's charms in a hushed, stained-glass voice. Then he said, matter of factly, "And now that I've told you an adult confidence, I expect you to treat it with adult respect. Don't go blabbing it around."

"You didn't have to say that," I told him. "Of course I won't tell anybody."

He continued to talk about her, about the time she was Miss Harvest Home and rode through town on a truck with pumpkins, when she sang "America, the Beautiful" at the Fourth of July picnic, and when she and Obie Biller won the dance trophy at the Moose

Club Frolic. But even though he remembered all these dates and places, he talked about Mary Grace as if she were a stranger. He talked about her like Roxanne and I might talk about Clark Gable, who was really something special.

"Roman," I told him, "I just don't think you realize how Mary Grace really is. You ought to talk to her more."

"I intend to," he said with a twinkle in his eye. "I may just drop by tonight."

Our days really began after supper. Because of the heat, we were eating late, after "Amos 'n' Andy" even. Then Mama and Mrs. Budd went from room to room, raising blinds and opening windows, and Grandpa went out to water the roses. Mary Grace began choosing her costume for the evening and Fred struggled up from the spirea bush. The whole household came to life.

After dark, we moved outside and stayed until the mosquitoes chased us in. It was a pleasant time. There was always company and the clang of horseshoes against the post and great bursts of laughter from the croquet court. The game was for adults only, but Pidd and I didn't mind. We were playing Red Rover and Prisoner's Base and Redlight with the kids from down the street. Mary Grace had her friends on the side porch. They were trying out new dance steps to the phonograph and breaking into giggles when they got mixed up.

Grandpa usually had a group of older men around him discussing the state of the world. They talked about Hitler taking over Czechoslovakia and the Italians going into Albania, and they ticked off countries that had fallen to this or that dictator. War is inevitable, they said. I could have told them that Prime Minister Neville Chamberlain of Britain and our own President Roosevelt wouldn't allow such a thing, but of course I didn't dare.

Mama seemed to perk up in the evenings, too. Some ladies from the neighborhood sat with her in the gliders and high-back wicker chairs, and they talked about quilt patterns and recipes and programs at the church. Mrs. Budd was usually playing croquet with the men or chasing around with us playing frozen catchers or some of the easier games, so Mama had her friends to herself.

I think it was hard for Mama to have Mrs. Budd with her all the time. I know she resented the fact that Mrs. Budd and Daddy were such good friends, and now Pidd was running to "Miss Sadie," as he called her, every whipstitch. I could understand why he did, all right. Mrs. Budd was always jolly, she fixed him between-meal snacks which he wasn't supposed to have, and she listened to his dumb jokes. Mama really didn't have time to do these things. The more work she had to do, the crosser she became; and the crosser she became, the more often Pidd ran to Mrs. Budd. It didn't seem fair, but that's the way it was.

I got to thinking all this while we were playing Hide-and-Go-Seek. I'd climbed the wild cherry tree by the side fence, and though Pidd passed under me a half dozen times, he never once looked up. I thought about how much Daddy was gone from the house and how Grandpa was interested in Mrs. Fingerle. I thought about Mary Grace riding around with Herschel and how I was always off with Roxanne or going over to help Roman. Who was left to pay attention to Mama?

Instead of running home free, I sneaked to the house and into the kitchen. I found the biggest tray we had and spread it with the linen cloth that was hemstitched around the edges. Then I made a big pitcher of lemonade and sliced lemons to float on top. I put ice in the tall cut-glass goblets that Mama used for company, and then as an afterthought ran outside by the downspout, grabbed a handful of mint, and added a sprig to each glass. When I stepped back to survey the tray, I had to admit that Mary Grace couldn't have done it better. Then I carried the whole thing out to the front porch and deposited it on the round wicker table in front of Mama.

"It's so warm," I said, "I thought you ladies might like something cool and refreshing."

I saw that my mother was startled, but she was nice enough not to say so. "Thank you, Vonnie. That was thoughtful of you." She gave me a special smile.

"Edna," Mrs. Crenshaw said, "It's hard to realize that you have two grown girls. I'm afraid I thought of LaVonda as a child, but here she is serving us, as nice as you please."

"Yes, it's hard to realize that Vonnie's growing up."

I left then, and would you believe it? That brother of mine wasn't even trying to find me. Almost everybody—our age, anyway—had gone home, and Pidd and Roxanne were sitting on the grass playing mumblety-peg. I was settling beside them when Roman came up, just as he said he would.

Mary Grace's gang had gathered out of sight of Mama and her friends on the front porch and the croquet grounds on the far side of the house. The girls danced together—the boys in our town were still working in the mountains—while Herschel changed the records. I suppose he felt it wouldn't have been polite to dance with Mary Grace when her friends didn't have partners.

Roman wasn't that polite. He walked onto the porch just as Herschel put on "Deep Purple." He grabbed Mary Grace, spun her around to face him, and off they danced. I decided then and there that there is a difference between doing a dance and dancing. The girls with their jitterbugging had been doing a dance; Mary Grace and Roman were dancing. The music was a part of them, and they dipped and whirled and swayed as though they were feeling and not thinking. Roman held Mary Grace close and they looked at each other, but neither smiled.

I think I've never seen a prettier sight than those two dancing in the half shadows—Mary Grace with her white skirts swirling around her legs, Roman so dark and lean and masterful. Nobody said anything; there was just the music and the light brush of footsteps and the swish of chiffon. After the music stopped and the arm of the phonograph swung over and clicked into its resting place, both of them stood still for a moment, as though they needed time to cast off the spell. Then they broke apart, and everybody started talking and laughing at the same time. Mary Grace looked immediately in Herschel's direction, but he had disappeared.

A wind came up then, promising the much needed rain, and we all scattered to fold up the canvas lawn chairs and bring in the croquet set. Our neighbors scurried home before the first drops fell, and the rest of us brought in the glider cushions and carried glasses to the kitchen. Daddy had turned off the outside lights and we were all standing on the porch listening to the thunder and waiting for the rain when we realized that nobody had seen Roxanne and Mrs. Budd for some time.

"Do you think they could have gone to their new house?" Mama asked.

My dad said he didn't think so, since there was no electricity.

"Were they with Herschel?" Mary Grace asked. She sounded anxious.

Pidd remembered seeing Herschel walk off alone, and Daddy said a man could take care of himself, but a girl and a woman . . .

Mama, who was never completely at ease until everybody was in and locked away for the evening, dispatched Pidd to recheck the upstairs rooms and me to circle the outside of the house. I called repeatedly until the rain sent me scurrying in.

Daddy had checked the sheds and hadn't found the Budds; Pidd and Mama hadn't found a trace of them in the house. We were all uneasy now, wondering whether we should call Roman at the Becketts or whether we should wait a few minutes.

After all, Mrs. Budd was a grown woman and we didn't like to interfere. On the other hand . . . We decided to call.

Mama was the one who finally found them. She had the phone book in her hand and was trying to find her glasses when she heard a muffled whimper from under the table. There, huddled together, big-eyed and rigid, were Roxanne and Mrs. Budd. They had clasped each other tightly, and Mama could not get them to come out from their hiding place or to release their hold on one another.

I tried to coax Roxanne. "Come listen to the radio with me," I said. "We can catch 'Lights Out.' You know I'll get scared if I listen all by myself." There was no response.

Daddy made a half-hearted attempt to pull them out, but he was a gentle man and hated to use force, especially on company. Roxanne and Mrs. Budd only held each other more tightly.

Finally, Mama crawled under the table with them. She motioned us out of sight, but we could still hear. "I didn't realize," she said, " how bad the first storm must have been for you. To have lain in that ditch and watched your house blow away must have been an awful thing. You didn't realize it yourself, Sadie. Not then. You had to take care of Roxanne, and then you had to be jolly and helpful because you were living here. You held back too long. But no matter. We're all here and we're concerned, and I'm going to stay right here with you until you want to come out."

Mrs. Budd began to cry very quietly, and Mama said, "That's fine. You just cry all you want to. You'll feel better. Now let me tell you again, this is just a harmless little old summer shower. You know how the garden needs rain? It'll all be over in just a few minutes. There's not even any wind now. Just a steady, soft, drizzle. Steady and soft. Nice and easy."

She went on to tell them how fine their new house would be, and how Mrs. Budd should take her insurance check and start shopping for new furniture, and had she thought about curtains for the kitchen. She asked Roxanne what color she wanted her room painted, and wasn't it grand that she could have a room of her own.

Daddy let Herschel in and put a warning finger to his lips. Then he tipped over and closed the kitchen door so Mama and the Budds could have their privacy.

Suddenly we both got a good look at Herschel. His coat was torn, there were scraped places on his cheek and chin, and his eyes were puffed and blue looking.

"What happened to you?" Daddy asked.

"I don't really know. I decided to take a walk about an hour ago and was just ambling along, minding my own business, when a car pulled up and three men—young men or half-grown boys, I don't know—jumped out and started dragging me to the sidewalk. I did what I could, but there were three of them and I must have passed out. They were gone when I came to."

"Did they take your wallet?"

"No, that's the strange thing. My wallet was still intact . . . and my watch. Even a ring I had in my pocket. An old family piece worth a great deal, I should think."

"Is there any way you could identify them?"

Herschel shook his head. "I just caught a blur of arms and legs."

"You didn't hear them call anybody by name?" Daddy asked.

Herschel hesitated.

"Did they call *you* any names?" I asked.

"People tend to do that sort of thing when they're fighting," he said vaguely.

I hadn't heard too much name calling, my family being dead set against the practice. But I remembered hearing names over at Roman's when his friends came to help build the house.

"Did they call you a Hun or a Kraut?" I asked.

My dad looked at me in amazement.

Herschel avoided the question. "Look, I don't

want to alarm the ladies. I'll be fine after a night's rest." He tried to smile. "I do hope you won't say anything about this." He limped to his quarters just before Mama came out of the kitchen with the Budds. She was stroking their hair and patting them as she led them up the stairs.

Now I had two things not to say anything about: the swastika and Herschel's beating.

CHAPTER
7

Things went from bad to worse after that night. On September 3, England and France declared war on Germany, and all the talk around the house was war. Herschel thought it was just a matter of time until the mills would be mobilized for defense work, and he spent long hours making plans for such a change. He called New York and London, hurried in and out with briefcases and folders, and, in short, seemed like an entirely different person. He was no longer one of Mary Grace's agreeable young suitors; he was the man in charge.

His aunt was completely unsettled by the anti-German feeling in Elk Run. There was twittering and whispering wherever she went, and she was at a loss to understand how the porter at her plant had suddenly become superior to her. Strangely enough, it was Mrs. Budd who offered solace and support. "It's got to be hard for a lady in your position," she said. "You've always been top dog. But there's been plenty of talk about me—about anybody from the Bottoms, for that matter—and I tell you what you have to do. You just square your shoulders, look them right in the eye, and tell them all to go to . . ." She hestitated. "No, I guess you couldn't do that. That takes practice. But I'm telling you—just like I've told Roxanne and Roman—people don't walk all over you unless you let them."

Mrs. Fingerle nodded but still kept on twisting her rings. "I've come to the conclusion that I should go away."

"That's exactly what you should not do," Mrs. Budd said. "Your home is here. You're a naturalized American citizen. You have every right to live here. Besides," she added, "every place is the same. Anywhere you go you've got your gossiping old biddies and your dumb young punks."

Even Mama, who was always saying the meek shall inherit the earth, got involved in a set-to on Mrs. Fingerle's behalf. We were buying material at the dry goods store. Or Mama was buying. I was shifting from one foot to the other wishing she'd make up her mind before I got too old to wear sprigged dimity.

Gladys Banks was pulling out bolts for Mama and helping her feel the material. "Do you still have the German people with you?" she asked.

Mama said, "Gladys, you know as well as you're standing there that the 'German people' are Mrs. Fingerle and Herschel. Your husband works at the Fingerle Mills. Your boys are playing in that park out there, which was given to the town by old Mr. Fingerle, and that includes the bleachers and the lights and the foundation *and* the bandstand. Mrs. Fingerle has lived in this town twice as long as you have, and her people were here when yours came over from . . . from wherever it was. Yes, they are still with us and they are welcome to stay as long as they like because I've never had finer guests. I don't think I'll buy anything today, thank you very much."

With that—the longest speech I'd ever heard my mother deliver—she pulled me out of the door without once looking back.

I heard Mrs. Banks say before the door slammed, "Well, I just asked."

Roman was to leave for college on the tenth. After the night of the dance, Mary Grace seldom saw him alone. When they did find themselves in the same company, he used the occasion to nag her about going to school.

"I just got out of school," she'd say irritably.

"But with that voice, you ought to be in the School of Music. It seems almost sinful not to be."

"That's what I told her," Grandpa said. "I offered to arrange it for her. I know Dean Harper quite well."

"But I don't want to sing professionally," Mary Grace would say. "Just leave me alone."

Grandpa and Roman would shake their heads and say they just couldn't understand it.

It was a busy time for everybody. Roman's house was almost finished, and Mama and Mrs. Budd were making curtains and buying furniture for it. Grandpa and Pidd sodded their front yard and seeded the back, and Roxanne and I painted wicker chairs for their front porch. (Painting wicker is the most tedious, onerous work on God's green earth, and we felt like saints when we finished.) Mama was letting Mrs. Budd can the last of the vegetables to tide her over until she had a garden of her own, and we all had a hand in that.

Mama had become much more relaxed with Mrs. Budd ever since the night they'd both crawled under the table. She had also let up on Grandpa. She didn't watch him so closely or try to smother him with attention. I heard her telling Mrs. Budd that she had accepted the fact that Grandpa needed a female companion. "Sometimes one's offspring aren't enough," she said.

Mrs. Budd agreed. "I think the world and all of Roxanne and Roman, but there's times when I get to hankering after old Beecher, rotten as he is."

"How long has it been since you last saw him?" Mama asked.

"I imagine it's been eighteen, twenty months this time."

"I see." Mama was quiet for a long time.

"Yep"—Mrs. Budd clanged the lid down on a saucepan—"You're lucky to have a full-time husband, Edna."

"I suppose so. I remember when Matthew was away in the war."

"You all ought to get out more. Have a little fun while you can. Know what I mean?"

"Perhaps when the children go back to school," Mama said. "I think I'll scrub those potatoes before you put them in to bake."

"Good heavens, Edna. You'll wait your life away.

Go tonight. Matt can afford it. He ought to be raking in the jack with all this building going on."

"Twenty months is a long time, Sadie. I don't know how you manage."

I don't know what else was said, but Mama and Daddy did go out, and Mama looked especially nice. She was wearing a pink dress with a white ruffle at the neck and had arranged her hair in a fluffier, softer style. Her cheeks were flushed and her eyes were twinkling, and for the first time I saw where Mary Grace got her good looks. She was acting as silly as Mary Grace, too.

No, I had to take that back. Mary Grace used to be flighty, but she had changed over the summer. Now she was acting older than Mama. Even though the boys were drifting back to town after their summer's work, she didn't give them the time of day. She and Herschel went out a lot: to church, the movies, shopping, or just around. If Herschel walked out to roll up the car windows, Mary Grace went along. They had their own little private jokes and special looks, and just like Mama and Daddy, when either one of them came into a room, they unconsciously glanced around for the other.

Herschel didn't have a meeting on this particular night and Mary Grace had said, since he'd worked so hard all week, why didn't they just spend a quiet evening at home. (This did not sound one bit like the old Mary Grace.) Now they were having a good time—a hilarious time—looking through old photo albums and scrapbooks. He scooped up a picture of Mary Grace in curlers and tried to put it in his wallet, and she tried—not too hard—to get it back.

Grandpa and Mrs. Fingerle were playing cribbage and arguing over the count. Pidd and I played Rook against Roxanne and Mrs. Budd, and all of us half-listened to "Fibber McGee and Molly." Later on, we popped some corn and brought up root beer from the cellar, so all in all it was a pleasant evening.

Mama and Daddy came in, laughing and trying to tell us about this funny movie they'd seen, something with Abbott and Costello; they couldn't remember the name. Everybody was gathered around them hearing about the pie-throwing scene except Pidd. I happened to glance up and see him staring out the window, though what he could see with the lights on inside was beyond me. He moved a step closer as if listening; then there was a crash and a scattered tinkling of glass. Pidd screamed and fell to the floor, blood streaming down his face. Mrs. Budd, who was closest, went to him, but he turned away and said, "Mama?" and then fell unconscious.

CHAPTER
8

Mama knelt on the floor cradling Pidd's head, pressing the gash on his forehead with her white shawl. Mrs. Budd ran to the telephone. The rest of us stood looking down at Pidd in helpless rage.

It was my grandfather who found the rock with its crude note, now bloodstained: GET OUT OF ELK RUN. HITLER WANTS YOU; WE DON'T. With shaking hands, he turned the note this way and that and held it to the light. Mrs. Fingerle swayed toward him. "My fault," she said. He grabbed her with his free arm.

"Come, Marta; I need you." Still supporting her, he led the way to his study. "Roxanne, LaVonda, come."

He motioned us to sit around his desk, but I stood at the door looking out at Pidd. With Roxanne's help, he began to tear through a lifetime of files. I had helped organize them once; I knew he'd saved every note his pupils had ever written him, every crayoned picture of the First Thanksgiving, all the poems, history reports, and English themes worthy of being presented to Professor Comstock. There were also disciplinary writings on "Why It Is Important That I Do My Part in Keeping the School Clean" and "Ways in Which I Must Respect the Rights of Classmates."

"I'd know that handwriting, Marta. When I checked your other letters, I knew I'd seen those backwards Ns, the combination of small and capital letters, the lettering mixed in with cursive writing. But memory fails. We must check each folder against this last piece of venomous stupidity."

I could not do this. I had to watch Pidd. The doctor was cleaning his head, talking all the while to calm my mother. Grandpa, behind me, was automatically

discarding certain folders; "No, she moved to
Lansing, Michigan. No, he was killed in an au-
tomobile accident last Halloween." He called
Herschel and Mary Grace to help. Mary Grace looked
faint, and Herschel turned her face away from Pidd
and guided her across the room. I let them through.

The doctor was sewing Pidd's head, and I closed
my eyes until he was finished. Then there were
instructions about possible concussion, develop-
ments to be expected, and information on when the
doctor should be summoned. Daddy picked up Pidd
and carried him up the stairs, Mama following.

After they were out of sight and the doctor had left,
I began to cry. For some reason. I kept thinking of
Pidd sailing down the creek when the water was up,
and me running down the bank crying and him
going out of sight. I couldn't seem to stop crying
until Grandpa, in a harsh commanding voice, called
out, "Hush up, Vonnie. Get in here and stop
indulging yourself."

I did try to help but the words blurred together and
the content was so awful, I couldn't concentrate on
the handwriting. Roxanne, who was good at puzzles,
checked out her stack of folders against one of the
notes, then quietly took over my stack. Mary Grace
was dutifully helping Herschel, and he and my
grandfather were talking of legal matters: what

charges could be brought against the culprits and what possible punishments could ensue.

"It should never have gone this far," Herschel said angrily. "Aunt Marta, why didn't you tell me? I can't understand why you didn't tell me after that very first letter."

"You were starting a new career." Mrs. Fingerle spoke in a tired, flat voice that I wasn't used to hearing. "I didn't think you should be disturbed."

"Career be hanged. There's no reason good enough to let yourself be slandered."

"I'm an old lady," she said. "Hate campaigns can't hurt me much more. But if you'd interfered, these terrible people might have aroused sentiment against you. With your position at the Mills, I didn't think you needed hostility from the town."

"Oh Aunt Marta"—Herschel spoke more gently now—"I don't want that kind of protection from you. The price is too great."

"I did what I thought was best," she said. "But now, the little boy . . ."

Mrs. Fingerle had done her best, as she saw it. And Mama wanted the best for me and Mary Grace and especially, right now, for Pidd. Mrs. Budd wanted Roman and Roxanne to grow up strong so people couldn't walk all over them. All three women, though as different as three sassafras leaves, had one thing in common: They all wanted the best for their children, and they were trying as hard as they knew how to help them.

I guess that was an important thing about growing up. You had to learn to think about somebody other than yourself. That was hard. I'd been trying to put myself in other people's shoes all summer, and sometimes it was unpleasant and sometimes downright painful.

"No mistake about it," Grandpa said. He and Herschel were comparing hate notes with papers in a folder marked *Paradine Carr*.

My father's heavy footsteps clumped down the stairs. "Matthew," Grandpa called. There was a conference at the foot of the stairs, and I heard Grandpa say, "No, Matthew. No violence. We've had enough of that."

"Vonnie, go to your mother," Daddy said. "I'll be at Sheriff Thompson's. Call if there's any change with Pidd." Carrying the notes and the folder and the blood-stained rock, he and Herschel and Grandpa went out to Herschel's car.

Pidd lay unmoving on the white sheets. Mama held his hand and never took her eyes off his face.

"Has he come to?" I asked.

She shook her head.

We sat there in silence for what seemed like a year. Mama reached over once and with her free hand touched my cheek. "I'm glad you're here, Vonnie. You're such a comfort to me."

Pidd opened his eyes. "Tigers?" he said.

Mama was perplexed. She bent to hear better.

I said, "No tigers, Pidd. Fred chased them all away." Fred groaned from the hall just then, and Pidd smiled.

Mama thought he was talking out of his head and she was alarmed. I told her what he meant. "Who's Fred?" I asked him.

Then he said three beautiful words, "The dog, dummy."

Mama laughed and cried a little, and I lent her my handkerchief. When she was calm again, I told her what had happened downstairs and that Herschel was a bit miffed with Mrs. Fingerle's keeping the hate notes secret from him. I explained that Mrs. Fingerle had thought she was doing what was best for Herschel.

"She's always done that," Mama said.

I decided the time might be right for the question that had been nattering away at me all summer. "Herschel *is* Mrs. Fingerle's nephew, isn't he?"

"Yes, he is," she said. "He's the son of her sister."

There was a long pause, and I thought she was going to leave it at that, but finally she went on. "Mrs. Fingerle gave her husband a divorce so he could marry her sister, Frieda, because Frieda was"— Mama hesitated—"because Frieda was in a family way."

Mama was embarrassed to say "family way." I thought of how much more embarrassed Mrs. Fingerle must have been by the situation. There must have been talk. The people in our town looked unkindly on divorce, no matter what the circumstances, even in 1939.

"It was a bad time for her," Mama said. "Your grandfather was a great comfort to her then."

"What about Herschel? Why didn't he stay with his mother and Mr. Fingerle?"

"They were in England when he was born; there was a branch of the Mills there. There was a party, a boating party, and both of them were drowned. That was when Herschel was three or four months old, I guess. Anyway, Mrs. Fingerle went over, settled the estate, and brought him back with her."

I was too overcome by all these facts to comment.

"It takes a special person to do what she did," Mama said. "She has never mentioned Mr. Fingerle or Frieda in an unkind way, even though they treated her shabbily. She has never once complained about raising another woman's child. She did what was needed."

"That was the responsible thing to do," I said.

"And the loving thing." Mama smiled at me in a new way, as if we were friends instead of relatives. "I'm telling you this because you've grown up so much lately, Vonnie. I know you'll respect the confidence and perhaps knowing will help you to understand Mrs. Fingerle's reserve a little better. She's taken quite a fancy to you, by the way. She asked your father and me if you could be her travelling companion."

I started to squeal and then remembered Pidd and caught myself.

"Don't get too excited now. This will be after you finish high school. A long time in the future." She was quiet for a moment. "Well, maybe not so long. Not as long as I'd like."

Mary Grace came up after she had settled Mrs. Fingerle, and the two of us sat on Pidd's window seat watching for the lights of Herschel's car. I was reminded of the time after the storm when we'd sat on my window seat and talked about Roman Budd.

"I think Mama would let you go with Roman now," I whispered. Mama was reading to Pidd on the far side of the room, and I didn't want to disturb.

"Why do you think that?" she whispered back.

"Because he's not an *other* anymore; he's a *nice*."

Mary Grace looked confused for a moment, then she remembered our earlier conversation. "You've figured out how Mama decided who's which?"

"Yes, and it's really very simple. The people she knows are *nice*; the people she doesn't know are *others*. She knows Mrs. Budd and Roman so they're okay now and you can go out with him."

"That seems too simple, Vonnie."

"I think that has to be right, though. Mama's afraid of people she doesn't know. I guess she's afraid they'll bring us harm, so they get to be predatory monsters. But after they get to be around the house—like Mrs. Budd—then they become just plain people."

The Hardy Boys had been trapped aboard the smuggler ship, *The Black Parrot*, and we listened until Mama read them out of their dilemma. Pidd knew *The Twisted Claw* word for word, but the rereading of it seemed to take his mind off the hurting.

"Mary Grace," I asked, "don't you like Roman anymore?"

"I don't dislike him."

"Well, you seem to go out of your way to avoid

him. I can't understand that. He's smart and ambitious. He's going to be governor some day."

"I know you like Roman, Vonnie, and probably what you say is true. But that's the point. He's too ambitious. For me, anyway. I don't want to fight battles and lead crusades. I don't want to be pushed. All I want is to enjoy life. I want to have a nice home and entertain. I want to arrange flowers for the foyer and sing in the church choir and plant roses and stay in one place long enough to see them bloom."

"I think you can do all those things very well," I told her. Privately I decided that her kind of life would not be exciting enough for me. But then Mary Grace and I were always different.

"What about Herschel?" I asked.

She smiled dreamily. "He's kind, Vonnie. We enjoy the same kind of things. We laugh, we talk. We understand each other. He's just a dear man."

"Do you know he carries in his pocket a ring—a family heirloom—of considerable value?"

There was a sharp intake of breath. "You're not teasing, Vonnie? You're not making up stories? I know you and Roxanne sometimes let your imagination run away from you.'

"Of course I'm not teasing," I said huffily.

"Oh, Vonnie." She screeched and hugged me, and Mama looked up and shushed us. Soon afterwards, my dad came pounding up the stairs. Even when he tried to be quiet, the floor groaned. "It's all over," he said. "Everything's been taken care of." He looked very stern, and I was glad I was not the person he'd tangled with. Then he saw that Pidd was awake. He smiled, and I wasn't afraid of him anymore.

CHAPTER
9

Over the summer Roxanne had taught me to be aware of people's strengths and weaknesses, my own included. Having lost four hundred and twenty-seven kitchen matches in the course of the afternoon, I was now fully aware that I was no match for Roxanne's skill at poker. If I had two pairs, she had three of a kind. If I had three of a kind, she had a full house. She also had a strong will to win—a real need—which I lacked, and most important of all, she was shrewd enough to bluff. Try as I might, I never did learn how to bluff.

"Vonnie," she said, "Take my advice. Don't ever play for money." She slipped a rubber band around the cards and put them in the big floppy purse she always carried. "I hope you'll be all right in high school." She looked at me a long time. "With me not around, I'm afraid you'll let people take advantage of you. You take care, hear?"

"I'll be okay. You'll write, won't you?"

Roxanne was enrolled in beauty operator's school in Whitehall. My school would start on the twenty-first when the new wing was supposed to be completed. We promised to write and to visit each other on the weekends, but somehow I felt we'd be going our separate ways. Everything was changing. People were leaving; the war was closing in. Nothing would be the same again.

"I want you to have my *Little Women*," I told her. Although she was practically grown, she really liked that book. I couldn't understand why until she mentioned that it was the first book she'd ever read from beginning to end. "You always have your nose stuck in a book," she'd say, plodding ahead to the next chapter. "There must be *something* to reading."

I left Roxanne counting her matchsticks. Mama had said there'd be no birthday party if the guest of honor didn't come in by three o'clock to change those disreputable clothes she'd worn all summer. I didn't object too strenuously; it was clothes-wearing time again. The leaves had already turned, the nights were cool, and the garden had been sown with winter wheat. Fall was with us, although I have never thought of summer as really being over until school started.

My party would be the last picnic of the summer. Even if my birthday hadn't happened along, I think there would have been some kind of celebration. We all seemed to feel the need of marking the end of a special summer. Mama had been cooking for two days, my dad had laid planks across sawhorses to make tables, and Mary Grace had camouflaged the rough lumber with checked cloths and arrangements of chrysanthemums. Pidd had put watermelons to cool in the springhouse and Grandpa had the ice cream freezer ready to crank. The Budds and the Fingerles were in the process of moving out, but they helped when they could. Herschel, with Mary Grace offering advice, strung Japanese lanterns in the side yard, and Mrs. Budd barbecued ribs at her new house. Mrs. Fingerle had ordered an enormous cake from Whitehall.

Being the guest of honor, I was not allowed to help. I'd spent most of the last two days at the creek, catching up on my thinking and soaking up the last sun of the season. There was a lot to think about; so many things had happened over the summer. But, considering the season as a whole, I still wouldn't have wanted to miss it. Maybe high school would be like that, I thought. No matter how awful it was, maybe after I'd graduated I could say, "Well, I wouldn't have wanted to miss these past four years." Maybe growing up was that way, or "Life," I said dramatically to the kingfisher that swooped down at my feet. He squawked at me, and I laughed back for having been so serious on such a fine day.

But the quiet times were over; I had a party to get ready for. I kicked off my sneakers, now ripped and yellowed from a summer's wear and tossed them in the wastecan. My denim shorts had faded to a slate gray, and after considering the broken zipper and the strained seams, I threw them in, too. My new clothes had been laid out on the bed: the pink and white candy-striped skirt Mama had made from yards and yards of material, the starched eyelet petticoats on loan from Mary Grace, the white scooped neck peasant blouse, the strappy sandals.

Mary Grace ran me a bubble bath because it was my birthday, and later helped me dress. We'd become much closer over the summer, so much so that I didn't resent it when she offered to do "something" with my hair. She pulled the front half of it off my forehead, secured it with rubber bands, and added a flat velvet bow. The rest swung loose around my shoulders. After surveying her handiwork, she said that my tan made my hair look almost black and also made my eyes look bluer, and with the dark lashes, I was striking. Mary Grace was an authority on such matters so I saw no reason to disbelieve her.

"Oh Vonnie"—she gazed off into space with the brush in one hand—"this has been the most wonderful summer in my whole life." She studied the engagement ring Herschel had given her, turning it this way and that to catch the light.

"You mean things are wonderful *right now*?" I asked.

"Oh, I wish time would stand still." She closed her eyes for a moment and sighed. "If there should be war, and Herschel would have to go . . ." She left the sentence dangling, then briskly changed the subject. "I suppose Mama will depend on you a lot when I'm gone. You'll be the big sister now."

We thought about that, and we decided we were both half-sad, half-happy about my new position in the family.

The Fingerles and the Budds—except for Roman—came to my party along with neighbors carrying covered dishes, and cousins from out of town. Many people brought extra guests—friends or relatives who were visiting. There was one boy there, Frank Randall, who would be in my freshman class at County High. He followed me around all afternoon, and it pleased me to think that I'd have at least one friend at school.

Wherever knots of men were gathered, there was talk about war. Canada had declared war on Germany on the tenth of September and some felt that it was just a matter of time until we joined the Allied forces. My dad was a strong isolationist, maybe because he had been in a war already. He had lots of arguments on that point since most of the younger men felt that we should jump in and settle the score once and for all. My dad never wavered in his position. "The last war was supposed to do that," he said.

There was also talk of Paradine Carr. "He just took off in the middle of the night," Miss Hattie said. "Loaded up that old rattle-trap car with two of his friends and headed north."

Miss Frances had heard that the sheriff paid Paradine a late visit that night.

"The defense plants are rolling up there. Maybe they planned to get jobs and make a killing," Chuffy's mother said.

All my mother said was "Good riddance."

There was a ball game in progress—sixteen to a side—which I didn't care to join since I was wearing Mary Grace's petticoats. While everybody was momentarily occupied, I took the opportunity to slip out past the garden, over the creek, and up the hill to the Budd house. Roman lounged against the big maple tree in the front yard, a book in his lap.

I stood looking down at him, my hands on my hips. "How come you didn't come to my party?"

"I had some studying to do," he said gruffly.

He dragged over a wicker chair for me, one Roxanne and I had painted, and another for himself.

"I don't believe you had that much studying to do," I told him flatly. "I think you didn't want to see Mary Grace. I think you're a sore loser."

His mouth hardened and he slapped angrily at a sweat bee.

"And you know what else I think?" I said.

"I imagine you'll tell me."

"I will indeed. I'm not afraid of you, Roman Budd. I think you never did love my sister. You never even thought of her as a person. She was just a prize you wanted to win, and that's shameless. You didn't even bother to find out what she was like; what kind of life she wanted to have, and . . ."

"Okay, okay. I get the message."

"Then stop sulking. You have six years of school ahead of you, and you know Mary Grace wouldn't have waited six years to get married, even if she liked you. At least *I* know that."

"You seem to be Miss Know-It-All today."

"You're not going to ruffle my feathers, Roman. I know you're smart, but so am I. You've got ambitions, but so have I. There's one thing I do know that I learned this summer that you don't know. You can't get so wrapped up in thinking about your own self that you ignore other people. No matter how all-fired noble your ambitions are."

"Are you quite finished?"

"I guess so. No, I'm not. I think it's awful of you not to come to my party when everybody else did." I blinked back tears and was angry at myself for losing control.

I don't think he noticed, and I was able to continue in a rational manner. "We had some good talks this summer. I thought we were friends." I got up, having said what I came to say. "I'd better get back before I'm missed. After all," I said sarcastically, "I *am* the guest of honor."

He got up too, and stood looking down at me. For the first time he smiled. Roman always looked like a different person when he smiled. I think few people ever saw him when he was being kind and gentle.

"What you say is right, Vonnie." He straightened my velvet bow. "You're a perceptive young lady, and that's a plus. You don't really have to be perceptive, as pretty as you look today."

That statement did ruffle my feathers and I blushed through my tan.

"You're going to be quite a woman, Vonnie Mercer." He laughed in a nice way and kissed me quickly, just barely brushing my lips. "Now, when I get to be an old, old man and you get to be the first lady President, I can brag to everybody that I gave LaVonda Mercer her very first kiss."

I heard shouts in the distance—"Vonnie? Vonnie?"—and I waved and took off running. All the way to the house I kept thinking: *When I am eighteen he'll be twenty-five. When I'm twenty, he'll be twenty-seven.*

"Vonnie," Daddy said when I reached the house. "The ice cream is finished. Come lick the dasher. It's your birthday."

Grandpa laughed and slapped my dad on the back. "You used to reserve that privilege when you were little."

When I'm twenty-two, he'll be twenty-nine. I licked the dasher with relish, being careful not to drip on my new candy-striped skirt.

June Lewis Shore

Elk Grove, Kentucky, and its citizens may be fiction, but June Lewis Shore has known and loved such communities and such people.

Mrs. Shore grew up in Jeffersontown, Kentucky, and earned a B.A. in English and art from Western Kentucky University in Bowling Green.

After living in Michigan and British Columbia, she is back in Jeffersontown as mother in a household that holds husband Ken, five active teenagers (who together play ten musical instruments, including the bagpipes), and an active St. Bernard named Sampson. Two-hundred-and-thirty-pound Sampson sings along with the bagpipes except during thunderstorms. Then, he sits in Mrs. Shore's lap.

The family has traveled around the United States and Canada in the little red school bus they have remodeled as a camper.

In addition to camping, fishing, and writing, June Lewis Shore enjoys painting, reading, baking—for which she has won ribbons, and collecting Indian and Eskimo sculpture. And June Lewis Shore enjoys people—like those in Elk Grove, Kentucky—for she sees them with kind and perspective eyes.